GRAPHIC NATURE

Daniel Damiano

Praise for GRAPHIC NATURE (2022)

"*Graphic Nature* tells a compelling story with interesting, believable characters while delivering a nuanced message that's both powerful and important. It also manages to involve the sagacity of life and death, love and loss, the sins of the father, and the indifference of God. You'll want to read it sitting down."
- Sunday's Mail

Praise for THE WOMAN IN THE SUN HAT (2021)

"While Daniel Damiano could have turned Peggy's tale into one of misery and desperation, he has instead crafted a humorous and uplifting story of perseverance and struggle against the odds."
- Seattle Book Review
(2021 Beach Read Recommendation)

"Daniel Damiano has written an extraordinary novel.- This is a novel that begins far away from where it ends and yet somehow brings together the strands of a woman's life in a way that is both breathtakingly beautiful and heart-wrenchingly painful."
– Notes from the City

"*5 STARS* - A wonderful and realistic novel that keeps you wanting more."
- The Authors Spot

Graphic Nature
© Copyright 2022 Daniel Damiano

Cover Illustration by Judy Alvarez
Cover Design by DD Paint

Published by fandango 4 Art House (1st Edition)

ISBN: 979-8-218-10469-6 (Paperback)

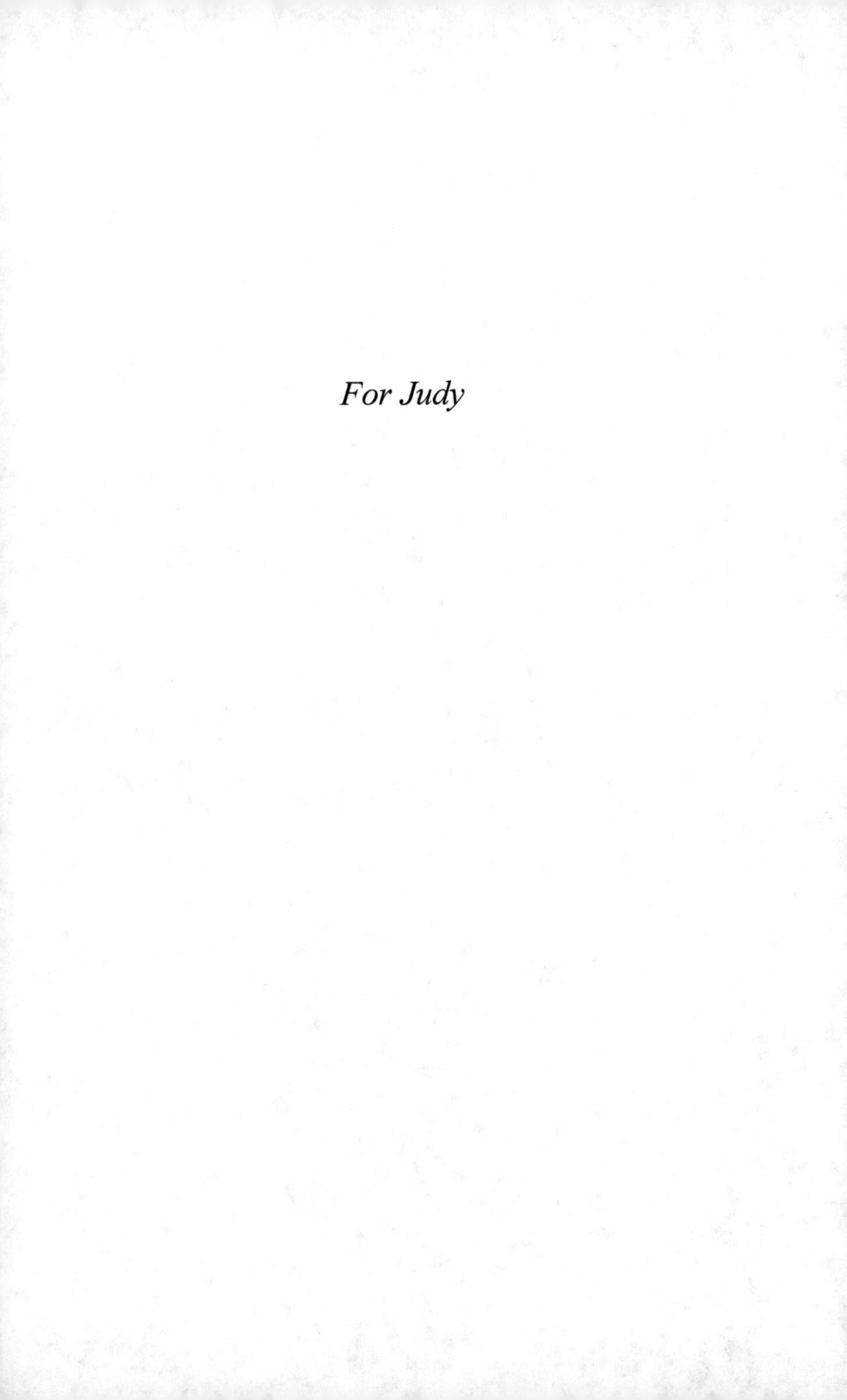

For Judy

Special Thanks

I wish to sincerely thank my friends and loved ones who lent their support and provided valuable feedback: Judy Alvarez, Lee Anderson, Ellen Barry, John Blaylock, Cinda Lawrence, Jack McCleland and Jannie Wolff.

1

~

Fontenay-sous-Bois - a suburb of Paris, France – 1880. Edmond de Capitoir was only a child then, but he still remembered. He remembered his father Albert's entrances into their humble residence after each assignment. He remembered the varying levels of fatigue in his father's face, depending on the length of his travels. He remembered how little his father spoke to his mother, as he removed his coat, scarf and hat, then sat down on the small wooden stool beside the door. It was this action that would result in the most vivid memory for Edmond: his father's shoes.

***

Paris, 1913. Edmond listened dutifully as he watched Alfred Ratier, the rather rotund Minister of Justice, spout with surprising clarity, despite the ample portions of marinated duck the minister was consuming at his desk. Edmond's unaltered professionalism would never cast the slightest judgment on Ratier's decorum, for Ratier was his superior, after all. He was the man who delegated Edmond's assignments throughout France. If there were adverse opinions that Edmond held regarding him, they were well concealed behind his façade that had been effectively unaltered in all his years with the Justice Department; a stark contrast to his younger brother and assistant Leopold, who often equated Ratier's physique to that of a walrus and his appetite to that of a wild boar. But Edmond prided himself on his ability to remove himself, for over the years his eyes had seen what most would deem unfathomable. Ratier's indulgences would be fairly tolerable by comparison.

And yet despite the dark sides of humanity that Edmond had been exposed to, his etiquette would be unrivaled, and seemed apt enough for a man with a personality that could be construed as somewhat rigid; even formal, with expressions of frustration or intolerance rarely displayed to even the slightest degree. And he was immensely clean. Clean to the point of envy by the most hygienic. It could even be speculated that surgeons likely did not sterilize their tools near the equivalent that Edmond cleaned his grooming items.

Now before Edmond was his stark dichotomy. Certainly not a man of ill repute. On the contrary, for Ratier was a high-ranking official, and was justly compensated. And perhaps it was just how much he was compensated that led to his gradually expanding girth. Yet despite his size and voracious appetite, he was always gregarious, and even boastful with Edmond. He would often keep him significantly longer than was needed, if just to regale with a story or a personal inquiry that Edmond was obliged to indulge. Regardless, Edmond felt he was only to be respected. Even as duck grease oozed down Ratier's chin like Gavarnie Falls, he could never not acknowledge this man as his superior. It was never a point of argument, despite Leopold's constant complaints to Edmond about his insufficient wages. In the end, as with previous ministers over the course of Edmond's tenure, Ratier was the provider of his opportunity. And what was Edmond, after all, if not the Chief Executioner?

"Versailles, on the 22nd of March, Edmond," Ratier spouted with his customary joviality, as he handed him the pertinent notarized documents, which granted Edmond official authorization to fulfill his assignment.

"Yes, sir," Edmond replied, as exact and economical as usual.

"And bring me back a dozen of those delightful éclairs from Maison's Patisserie while you're there, if you'd be so kind."

"Yes, sir."

"My Lord, they are positively succulent."

"Rumor has it, sir," Edmond forced the slightest smile, especially as he was not surprised by this request. Maison's certainly had a reputation in Versailles for their goods for many years, from breads to sweets. And while Ratier knew of the noted patisserie from his past travels, in his current esteemed position, he now had the opportunity to request that Edmond be the bearer of such sought-after delights when in Versailles. Ratier could also take comfort in knowing that, while Edmond was, of course, travelling for his profession, his utter reliability would assure that he would never forget his superior's indulgences. It could even be said that if Ratier had to rely on one thing, it would be Edmond's efficiency.

His acclaim for Maison's eclairs would continue to take precedence: "Oh, dear, the guilt that one receives from those succulent vessels can only be equated with a good Catholic missing church, but hopefully God's a little more forgiving in this regard," he snorted, accompanied by a momentary gagging from the duck he was still consuming.

"I'm sure He is, sir," Edmond replied, as his smile weakened.

"But are they not sumptuous, Edmond?"

"Oh, I can't say that you're wrong, sir, as I've never actually had them myself," Edmond said, as if trying not to offend.

"You've never had one?"

"No, I haven't, sir, but…they always look quite delectable."

"In all your trips to Versailles, you've never indulged?" Ratier spouted, in utter disbelief.

"Actually, no, sir."

"Well, you absolutely must!"

"Well,…"

"I'll insist that you try one this time, on my franc."

"That's very kind of you, sir, but I'm…I'm afraid I have an aversion," Edmond slightly stammered.

"An aversion?"

"Yes, sir."

"An aversion to what?"

"To custard," Edmond reluctantly replied.

"An aversion to custard?"

"Yes, sir."

"My God, man, you're French!"

"Yes, sir."

"Well, that's like a panda having an aversion to bamboo."

"It is unusual, I admit."

"Is this some sort of allergic reaction?"

"No, not really. Custard just tends to make me…rather nauseous."

"Well, I'm certainly sorry to hear that."

"Well, sir, it's not really cause for too much concern. There are worse things, yes?"

"Yes, I…suppose there are," and yet it appeared almost inconceivable to Ratier. To Edmond, it was somewhat ironic that Ratier, who doled out execution assignments with the ease of a Gin Rummy dealer, would be so taken aback by one's allergic reaction to something as seemingly innocent as custard. But for a man such as he, who felt justified in the many privileges that came with his title, such an aversion was a tragedy. This did not necessarily surprise Edmond, for in his observations from afar it appeared that, despite the accoutrements of family and lavish residences, true joy for officials of Ratier's standing seemed to only be obtained by diversions. Perhaps it was just another observation that made Edmond doubt the existence of a soul.

Once Ratier recovered from Edmond's stunning admittance, as if not wanting any more éclairs to go to waste, he would make an addendum to his order: "You know what, Edmond, you'd better make that *two* dozen."

"*Two* dozen éclairs, sir?"

"I know, I'm a cow," Ratier guffawed. "But my God, Maison's does have a particularly sinful touch."

"So I've heard," as Edmond returned a now strained grin, while making a notation.

"And three Milles Feuilles. My wife enjoys those very much."

"I see."

"Or, rather, she enjoys how much *I* enjoy them. I don't believe she much cares for them. At least help yourself to a Mille Feuilles, Edmond."

"Well, again, thank you, sir, but…"

"Of course. The custard."

"Yes, sir."

"Well, then how about one for your wife?"

"I'm not married, sir."

"Not married?"

"Correct, sir."

"Really?"

"Yes, sir," as Edmond's polite yet strained smile returned. For this would be far from the first time that he needed to remind the Minister of something he had previously disclosed to him. While it was obvious to anyone who had eyes that Ratier loved indulgence, it would be equally so only to those who needed to speak with him with some professional regularity that he could also possess the attention span of a flea. Perhaps this was genetic, or even a case of his dietary regimen beginning to seize his memory. Regardless, Edmond never would so much as sigh in private at the repetition he often endured as a result of his superior's personal inquiries. However, this was not to say that they didn't make Edmond feel all the more inferior, particularly with regard to his domestic background. For it was certainly not lost on him that a man of 45 years of age in France not having his own family would be deemed…unusual.

"Since when?" Ratier followed, regarding Edmond not being wed.

"Since…my birth, sir."

"Why did I assume you were?"

"I suppose because…many are."

"Yes, I suppose so," Ratier pondered, in the usual and similar fashion to his reaction of Edmond's custard allergy.

"Yes, sir," Edmond again forced a smile, as if his cheeks were two weak trees attempting to elevate a hammock, before Ratier's inquisitiveness quickly shifted back to his gluttony:

"In any case, Edmond, two dozen Eclairs…"

"And three Mille Feuilles," Edmond efficiently recited from his notation pad, on a separate page from the date and location details of his next execution.

"If you'd be so kind," as Ratier smiled. His appreciation for the pending delicacies taking precedence now over any official business.

"Of course, sir."

Edmond never so much as motioned to exit without Ratier's dismissal. While it would usually occur at this point, on this day, Ratier would keep him for a most unusual request:

"Oh, and, Edmond, when you return, we've arranged to have you meet with a journalist from *The Paris Herald.*"

"A…a journalist, minister?" a sudden jolt of nerves coursed through Edmond.

"He'll simply be asking you a few questions with regards to the state of capital punishment here," Ratier disclosed, with near apathy, as he glanced at the documents before him, with an alternating sip of Bordeaux.   But his comfort was now an even more stark contrast to Edmond's trepidation.

"Well,…with all due respect, sir,…why will he be asking *me*?"

"Oh, it's nothing to worry about, Edmond. I know you're not a man of many words and, therefore, we don't suspect that this will take up but a few moments of your time. However, we do feel that you will be a most appropriate representative."

Edmond audibly swallowed, as he continued to observe Ratier alternating between sips and glances at the papers before him. With a near obsequious hesitancy that would often accompany a question, "Well, again, with…all due respect, sir, do you feel that *I* am of a sufficient enough stature to be speaking to a newspaper on the Justice Department's behalf?"

Ratier managed to lift his head, as if finally acknowledging Edmond's reticence. "Most certainly, Edmond. You've been of considerable value to this department for many years. I assure you that you have my wholehearted endorsement." He went back to his paperwork, flipping pages with his grease-laden fingers almost randomly… All the while, Edmond stood before him. He did not wish to speak on this matter further, but understood his utter lack of recourse. He would go forward with a modicum of justification that he was being asked to represent his department for a, surely, rudimentary article.

And so, with a tepid grin, he conceded, "Well, …anything that I can do in support of the department, Minister."

"Very good, Edmond." He looked at Edmond again, smiled, "In the meantime, two dozen éclairs…"

"And three Mille Feuilles."

"Oh, you'd better make that *six*, Edmond!"

"*Six*, monsieur?" as Edmond quickly made the adjustment in his notes…

"I know, I'm awful," Ratier guffawed, "but I do have to take advantage of your Versailles excursions, as I don't get there myself much these days," his smile broadened, as nothing could incur such childlike whimsy in the man more than expectancy of treats.

"I understand, Minister".

"Have a safe journey, Edmond. I'm certain that everything will go smoothly, as always."

***

Various townspeople gathered outside Saint Pierre Prison in the crisp early March morning, to bear witness. Jean Paul Le Der was led out, his hands bound behind him. His face was predictably pale, lifeless before the life would soon be extracted from him. Those who watched were likely the same as those who witnessed the last public execution in Versailles. They were usually not people of considerable wealth, but more often proletariats – for who an event such as this would be considered a sort of escapism. The size of these crowds would usually amount to around twenty-five to fifty people, depending on the population of a particular city. If the population was smaller, chances are that most of a town would attend, since word would easily spread. And if there was enough boredom suffered by the local citizens, chances were likely that this would be considered the equivalent of an opera that they could not afford to attend.

To Edmond, they were all faceless and indiscernible, and he would have it no other way. He would never acknowledge their presence, for he would deem it disrespectful to his profession and to the procedure itself. It was clearly not a macabre performance for him, and he instilled this belief in those who worked alongside him: his younger brother Leopold, and Claude, a long-trusted crewman, now approaching 60 years of age, whose stomach for such work was the antithesis of Leopold's. By contrast, even after working alongside Edmond for much of his adult life, it appeared to never be a profession that Leopold truly adapted to, whereas Claude approached it as no different than a blacksmith or fishmonger. It was a job that he performed to Edmond's high standards, and one that he was able to move on from easily enough, as was evident in his sound sleeping on the train home afterwards or his voracious appetite, as if he hadn't just moments before witnessed a human head descend into a sawdust-filled bucket.

By now, Edmond's appearance was expected by the locals who had seen prior executions. His pronounced gallic mustache, black suit and top hat were recognizable to them, even as his name remained largely unknown. The only name that was known by the majority of those gathered would usually be the local clergyman who would recite prayer, if requested, and, of course, the convicted. In this instance, the latter was Jean Paul Le Der; a lifelong thief who appeared fated for no more than to be what he was. These details would be known mainly to the courts and to Edmond, who attended his sentencing, and would be documented in Edmond's journal.

The area would be relegated to a hush, seemingly quieter than a moment of silence during Sunday mass. The silence, in Edmond's mind, was the respect owed to the assailant whose fear was likely all-consuming, if not often displayed. Le Der, for one, did not express fear, but had already moved to a sad resignation. It was as if he had just witnessed a kaleidoscope of his life before him and, finally admitting that he had contributed so little to the world, could simply never fathom altering his criminal ways.

Claude and Leopold stood on either side of him, and gently assisted Le Der so that he was now lying upon the bascule. From there, Claude and Leopold slid him forward so that his head would now reside within the lunette, which would then be fastened. By now, the prayers from Father Louccaint would be faint, even as silent as the surroundings were:

"Our Father, who art in heaven, hallowed be thy name..."

As these words became more distant, the sounds of the guillotine being secured would resonate like a giant mallet against a train rail, accompanied by the omnipresent gloom of the gray sky. Leopold covered Le Der's head with a sack that allowed just enough space for him to breathe, despite the fact that he would not be breathing much longer. He looked at Claude, whose face never deviated much from that of a wrinkled rural landscape, unmoved and stoic. Leopold, in turn, looked back down at Le Der's covered head, looked up at the impending blade, then over at Edmond, who gave his usual final inspection of the device. All of this done without a word spoken, for Edmond asserted early on in his career at the helm that if everyone had done their jobs aptly, speaking would merely serve as evidence of amateurism, in addition to the unsettlement of the perpetrator.

Edmond stepped back, looked up at the blade, then down at Le Der…and, in two swift movements, approached and then pulled the lever – *WOOSH!* - followed by a dull thud, which would indicate that the head had swiftly fallen into the insulated bucket, otherwise referred to by Claude as the "head catcher", much to Edmond's consternation. Within minutes, Claude and Leopold would manage to remove the body into the adjacent basket, then the head and bucket, before cleaning and dismantling the machine, all under the observation of Edmond. Much of the locals would remain until the device was completely removed, which often confounded Edmond. *It's as if they want to get their money's worth, without having spent a cent*, he often mused.

***

Leopold and Claude were assigned with preparing the device for transport on the next train back to Paris. While this was being done, Edmond had set aside just enough time to venture to Maison's Patisserie to fulfill Ratier's culinary request.

As in previous visits, he shyly peeked through the window and looked inside. He expected whom he would see, but wanted to take as much time as he could to simply observe her without the distraction of his own nerves. Her name was Juliette, a name still as yet unknown to Edmond – as his was unknown to her. She was the daughter of the owner, Maison himself. Maison was usually out of sight to the public, both due to the fact that he was the primary baker and also because, at least from the occasional bellows of frustration that would emanate from the kitchen, he did not appear desiring of social interactions. That much he appeared to have in common with Edmond, whereas his daughter Juliette, while somewhat shy, could not help but radiate kindness – and she had never failed to appear warm and welcoming to Edmond whenever he frequented. After several visits, over the past three years in which Ratier was the Minister of Justice, Edmond's attraction to Juliette had only increased, and yet his ability to move beyond the formalities of their exchanges in the shop remained utterly daunting to him.

After watching her write in a small book behind the counter for several minutes, Edmond finally entered, as there was not much time left before he and his crew's train was to depart from Gare de Versailles, just blocks away. He had his customary walking stick in hand, which would sometimes serve as a literal crutch that he needed when speaking to her. The ignited bell from the opened door would prompt Juliette to quickly hide the book and lift her eyes, as Edmond approached.

"Good morning, madame," he managed confidently enough.

"Good morning, monsieur," Juliette smiled.

"It always smells so wonderful in here."

"Yes, I know. I feel I gain pounds by that alone."

"By the smell?" Edmond asked, unaware of her jest.

"Oh, yes."

"Well, it…it certainly doesn't show," he managed, with an awkward seriousness. It was quickly becoming clear that, as the opening formalities were subsiding, so would gradually fade any comfortability in Edmond's conversation.

"Oh, well. Thank you," Juliette smiled again, though this time there appeared to be something else there. It wasn't discernible to Edmond, other than the possibility that she remembered him. *Does she?* he wondered. He never assumed.

As he asked this to himself, it soon became apparent that there was only silence between them, and he was staring at her…

"Do you see anything that you like?" she asked.

"Anything…?" Edmond swallowed hard, as his cane, its handle now wet with perspiration, slipped from his hand and descended to the floor. He immediately grabbed it and nervously resumed his perfect posture, as if unwillingly posing for a portrait. "Oh, yes. Yes, of course. I'm…" as he pulled out his small writing pad, and quickly flipped past his notes relating to Le Der's execution before coming upon Ratier's pastry list. "I'm to bring back several items, if you'd be so kind."

"Of course."

"Thank you," as his hand shook slightly. "Now let's see here. Two dozen of your famous éclairs…"

"Yes."

"And six Milles Feuilles."

"Very well," she sustained her smile, as she pulled a small pastry box from a nearby stack, and ducked to retrieve the displayed pastries that sat in perfect alignment, like a decadent metropolis. Edmond would take the opportunity of her face being momentarily obscured to gather himself, as he realized his heart was slightly palpitating. He quickly took several slow breaths while, at the same time, dabbing his moistening forehead, and felt that he was at least sufficiently masking his unease, which could only have been apparent.

As Juliette continued to pull one of the many requested eclairs from the display case, Edmond sauntered slowly to the window, both to help in offsetting his nerves and to possibly garner a subject for a semblance of conversation:

"The clouds are out yet again, it seems," he said, too softly.

"I'm sorry?" Juliette peeked over the counter.

"Oh, I'm… The clouds!" he said, too loudly.

"Yes?"

"I was just…noting that they're out again."

"Yes. It seems so," as she waited with some expectancy, before turning her attention back to the éclairs.

Edmond looked at her, then back out of the window at the relatively quiet Rue Chablés of the early morning, "Were you planning to venture out today?"

He felt the halting of her motion, as his eyes remained on the momentarily bare sidewalk.

"I wasn't, actually. I'll likely only have much of a desire to read on my sofa, I'm afraid."

He turned to find her standing with the opened box in hand, surprised of her commitment to his banal inquiry.

"I see. Well, there's…certainly nothing wrong with that," he replied through his forced grin. And to his further surprise, she would expand on this: "I've…always enjoyed the places that words can take me. A teacher of mine once said that if it's raining out, one may be transported to a sundrenched hillside on any given page."

"Yes, well,…that is unless one is reading Dostoyevsky," even Edmond was surprised at the quickness of his retort, almost as if it emanated from another mouth.

"I'm afraid I've avoided him. From what I've gathered, I don't believe he ever even *saw* the sun," she replied, with an unexpected shyness, which served to instantly make Edmond regret his attempt at humor.

"Yes, well,…quite possibly," he barely uttered.

As yet another awkward silence between them developed, Juliette's response served to confirm all the more Edmond's feeling that the harshness of the world was something she may have been keeping at bay. But, of course, he could only speculate that this was true and, if so, what its roots were. What exposure had she had to the darkness of human nature that Edmond, by way of his trade, had long been aware of?

"I'm sorry, would you like the éclairs in a separate box?" Juliette brightly shifted, the suddenness taking Edmond by surprise, before he adjusted. "Yes, thank you."

As Juliette tied up both boxes with an efficiency that Edmond could only admire, "Your family is certainly in for a treat. These are our most popular."

Edmond was, again, taken aback. This time it was by her assumption of his marital and family status. She had never said this before. His breath was slightly ahead of the words he wanted to quickly emit to assure her that he was, in fact, a bachelor. Time was now very much of the essence, as he couldn't help but envision Leopold and Claude at Gare de Versailles awaiting his arrival. And yet, he did not know when he would see her again. These excursions were a brief moment of a life that had largely been void of a social component, which Edmond long believed was unnecessary. But his mere glance through the window of Maison's would challenge this philosophy, resorting him from a committed representative of France's Justice Department to that of a perspiring, tongue-tied middle-aged man now besieged by a near arrhythmia.

"Oh, I don't... These aren't for my... I don't...have a family...of my own."

"Oh, I'm sorry. I mean, to presume…" she replied, accompanied by a slight blushing in her cream-colored cheeks.

"Oh, no,…not at all."

"A soiree, of sorts?" as Juliette attempted to recover from her previous inquiry.

"What…what makes you ask?" Edmond smiled, intrigued by her curiosity.

"Well,…the quantity, really."

"Oh. Yes, it is…rather considerable, isn't it," he smiled again, observing the boxes.

"Well, for one."

"Even one twice the width of myself."

Juliette laughed, and such a reaction was most unexpected if certainly embraced by Edmond, who considered himself most fortunate that anything he would say would generate something other than unsettled grinning or outright embarrassment. With their mutual laughter then came a sort of momentary courage: "Actually, they *are* all for me," Edmond boasted.

"Are you serious?"

"Oh, I'm deathly serious about pastries, madame. Why, my doctor prescribes them."

"What?" Juliette grinned, never having heard anything so absurd.

"Oh, yes. He says that pastries help build the immune system which can help fight a variety of maladies."

"Oh, really."

"Oh, yes."

"Such as?" now keenly aware of Edmond's jest…

"Well, polio, for one," Edmond proceeded. "The plague. Diptheria. German measles. The list is quite extensive. Of course, keep in mind that I'll die of a heart attack long before I acquire any of these ailments, but I believe that's the point."

"How very funny."

"Well,…" Edmond relished her amusement, but now feared just how he could resume beyond this jovial exchange. He looked at her, then down at the counter, then at the two boxes before him…before returning his eyes to hers, as if the jester had departed and left him to his usual devices. "Actually, these…are for an associate of mine."

"Oh," she followed, a certain embarrassment returning to her. "Well, good for him. Or her."

"Him," Edmond corrected.

"I see," which brought a smile to her.

"A rather…*ample* him," a well-submerged slip that again surprised him.

"Oh. Well,…*more* to see," Juliette returned. The quickness of her reply swiftly thrust them into mutual laughter. Edmond's caution at revealing a public opinion about Ratier's girth now was distant to his developing comfort with her…

"I…I have an aversion," he then confessed.

"An aversion?"

"Yes."

"An aversion to pastries?"

"Well, to custard, in particular."

"Is that so?"

"Yes. That is…true," his admittance now on the verge of becoming an embarrassment to him, seeing as Juliette appeared to find such an aversion as unusual as Ratier.

"Well, I'm sorry to hear that. I mean, one thing that you can't allow yourself."

"Yes, well…I suppose it is, but…there are worse things, aren't there?"

"Yes. I'm certain there are," Juliette slightly smiled. Her response did not hold the judgment that Ratier's did. By contrast, she seemed to understand all too well. "Myself, I haven't had a pastry of any kind in over 20 years."

"No!"

"Oh, yes. And I've worked here since the age of 9."

"Really," replied Edmond, stunned.

"Yes. Well, it's my father's establishment, passed on from my grandfather."

"I see. Well,…your will is astonishing, considering your tempting surroundings."

"Yes, well, at the same time, I don't suppose it's all that unusual when you've had constant exposure to the same thing over a lengthy period, yes?"

"No. I suppose not."

The awkward silence appeared again, filled by their mutually uncomfortable smiles, and the occasional murmured cursing from Maison in the kitchen, which would often come and go like subtle ripples, along with the sporadic clangs from the metal trays. Edmond nervously rubbed his forefinger along one of the pastry boxes, while clenching his cane handle, searching for his next words…

"Will there be anything else?" she asked.

Edmond's cane nearly slipped from him again, but this time he would not let it get away, as he weakly smiled, "No, that…that will be all." He quickly placed three francs on the counter, "And could you please provide me a receipt for these?"

"Of course."

Juliette provided his change and then began writing out Edmond's receipt, which he would of course return to Ratier for reimbursement. As he observed her elegant handwriting, he honed up a last bit of courage: "It's…it's nice to see you again."

She stopped writing, then looked up at him. "Me?"

"Yes. I'm…I'm sorry, you probably don't recall me from your many patrons."

"No, of course, I…I remember you. It's been some time since your last visit, hasn't it."

"Um…yes, several months, I believe."

"Are you *from* here?"

"Versailles? No.   Paris, actually. Saint-Fargeau. That's where I reside, currently."

"Oh, I see," she smiled, then returned to complete Edmond's receipt. "Here you are."

He took the slip of paper from her hands gently, wanting to somehow stop time or slow the seconds that were becoming minutes. He pocketed the receipt, gathered the boxes, then began towards the door…

"It was nice seeing *you* again," she returned.

He froze with the boxes clutched to him, momentarily breathless. "Oh. Yes, well. You really have…a lovely establishment here. It's always a pleasure to come to."

"Despite your aversion," she said, seeming more intended as a compliment than a jest.

"Well, sometimes…one need only his sense of smell to be satisfied, as you…aptly mentioned."

As Edmond said this, it became clear to him that he meant something very different. And it seemed as though she knew that as well. He waited for her to respond beyond her smile, but, instead, all he would hear was the distant train whistle summoning him.

***

2

~

They sat beside each other on the train back to Gare du Nord. The pattern of this trip would deviate little from most of the professional travels that Edmond, Leopold and Claude would embark on together. Claude would be sleeping soundly, his snores reliably severing the air. Edmond would look ahead, with an occasional glance out at the passing landscapes, while Leopold would fiddle in his seat, and usually expel a quip of some kind in the hopes of engaging Edmond into a semblance of conversation, which rarely occurred.

As Leopold observed the boxes upon Edmond's lap, "What'd he get *this* time?" he asked, if somewhat knowingly.

Edmond stared ahead, and without humor, "Twelve éclairs and six Mille Feuilles."

"Dear God, and he'll eat them all himself, the gluttonous sow," Leopold murmured, turning back to the window he sat beside.

"Yes, I suppose he will," Edmond replied, in his usually rigid delivery that was all the more pronounced when his brother attempted humor or a harsh, if obvious, observation regarding their employer.

Leopold continued to stew, as he watched several idle cows staring back at him. "Every time we venture there, he has to have his precious sweets from Maison's. If I wasn't sick to my stomach, I'd eat one just as a show of rebellion."

"Well, that wouldn't be very courageous of you, Leo, considering that *I* am the one who will be presenting the boxes to him."

"Well, hell, *you* should eat one then. You certainly have the stomach."

"I've no desire to vent your hostility towards Ratier with thievery," as Edmond remained looking ahead.

"It's a bloody pastry, Edmond, which he doesn't even pay for with his own money. *'Thievery'*. My God, everything is a federal judgment with you. Wake up Claude. *He'll* eat one."

"Leo, that's enough."

"I don't know how the hell he does it. Eats and sleeps soundly before and after without even flinching."

"You would do well to rest your eyes yourself, Leo."

"Since when have you seen me sleep on a train?

"Well, I certainly wish you'd start."

Leopold looked at Edmond, who remained gazing ahead. Their exchanges for the majority of the time in which Edmond had held his post went similarly, except there was unquestionably a developing unsettlement in Leopold that Edmond was loath to acknowledge.   While it did little to interfere with them professionally, it made their personal relationship increasingly challenged, if not outright formal. And yet, somehow, Leopold always seemed to have a hope that he could crack his older brother's exterior, if not slightly loosen his tie.

"At least let me take one for the boys," as Leopold reached for one of the boxes…

"No, Leo!"

"We'll blame it on the clerk."

"Absolutely not," Edmond barked in a hushed tone, forever cognizant of his surroundings.

"*Fat*ier will not miss one damn pastry, Edmond."

"Obviously, you don't know *Rat*ier as I do. He'll take inventory."

"My God, he has nothing better to do than count sweets? He sits behind his desk, playing holier than thou and doing nothing of significance except watching his rump expand. The least he can do is throw a nice little crumb to his subordinates, which isn't much more than our salary."

"I'm aware of my salary, Leopold."

"Are you aware of *mine*? I make less than you."

"That's because you're my assistant, Leo. And I don't make much more."

"So why don't *you* complain?"

Edmond looked at Leopold, "Why don't *you*?"

"Because, for one, the cow doesn't even know my name after 3 years. *Leonardo*, he calls me."

"I'm aware of his selective memory…"

"And also because you're my superior and can, therefore, speak on my behalf,…as well as your own."

"I'm not going to put myself in that position right now, Leopold."

"What position? I'm not asking you to place your head in the lunette, for heaven sakes."

"Leo, please!"

"Didn't father speak for you when you assisted him?"

"He didn't need to."

"You spoke for yourself?"

"I didn't speak at all. I wasn't dissatisfied."

"But you are *now*."

Edmond looked at Leopold, clearly taken aback by such an observation: "I've never complained to you about my salary."

Just as quickly, Leopold regretted his statement, but could not resist an admittance: "Then…I must have read it," as Leopold turned again to the window, knowing well what would follow, as Edmond, for the first time, fully turned his focus to him.

"Read it where?" he intensely whispered.

Leopold caught sight of a passing abattoir, which only added to his reluctant admission. "In your journal."

"What the hell were you doing reading my journal?!" Edmond could only yell as loud as a whisper would let him.

"Edmond,…"

"That journal is solely for my own eyes. It is not for public consumption."

"Edmond, I'm not the public. For Godsakes, I'm your brother."

"You're not *me*. Therefore, that makes you the public. That's professional documentation."

"Well, we are in the same profession."

"I don't care, Leopold. You invaded my privacy. And you didn't know it was professional until you read it. As far you knew, it was personal divulgences, and that's no less an invasion."

"I apologize, alright? We had a long train ride back from Bordeaux last month and I had nothing to read."

"How did you manage to sneak my journal."

"I didn't 'sneak' it, Edmond. I simply…gandered at it when you went to stretch your legs."

"You're pathetic."

"I won't do it again, alright…?"

"42 years old, a wife, children, and you're as infantile as ever. If our father were alive, you'd be over his knee."

"You'd think I'd be over his knee at 42 years of age?"

"Don't ever read my journal again. *Ever.*"

Edmond had rarely outwardly expressed such indignance to Leopold, but it was of little surprise considering the importance his journal held for him, which he usually kept in his interior pocket on longer trips – otherwise, he would more often document his entries in the privacy of his residence. Since Edmond had obtained the role of Chief Executioner, he had made it a point to record his assignments, which was unusual considering it was something that his father had never done. It certainly wasn't required of his profession, for Ratier and the Justice Department would not care to hear Edmond's observations regarding his executions other than that they were performed successfully. But, somehow, it became necessary for Edmond. The journals would largely contain entries regarding the persons he were to execute, usually beginning with information he obtained during their sentencing. They would include the crime or, more often, crimes of the accused, and any background information he accrued which, often he felt, would indicate possible motive or establish the roots of one's unlawful behavior. Rarely would there be a personal revelation, as would normally appear in one's diary. However, on occasion, something could possibly seep out – such as a few, brief recent entries in which Edmond noted how it'd been years since he had received a raise in his salary.

Edmond gazed out bitterly, as Leopold observed him, regretfully. "I didn't read much. Just…a paragraph. I've just always been curious what you wrote in there. I mean, God knows you never tell me anything, so I thought I'd find out something."

"What the hell are you, a detective? Find out what?"

"Nothing salacious, Edmond. Just, say, if you had a…particular female companion. Michelle always asks."

"Why?"

"Because she's concerned."

"And why is she concerned?"

"You know women; *a man alone is a lonely man*. At least that's what she feels."

"Or what *you* tell her."

"I don't tell her any such thing, Edmond. I don't *know* anything."

"I'm not lonely at all, Leo. So let's please leave it at that."

As a conductor swept by, Edmond resumed his gaze ahead, hoping that Claude's adjacent snoring and the train's engine would be the only sounds that he would hear for the duration of their trip.

"*Of course*, you're not lonely. There's Theresa," Leopold couldn't resist, as he looked out his window.

"Leo, enough, please."

"Is there anyone *aside* from your pet turtle?"

"Leo, if I haven't mentioned something to you or documented it for you to deviously gander at, it does not mean that it doesn't exist. It's merely…a subject which I choose not to speak about. Now, please."

Leopold took a moment to digest this, hoping, if not necessarily believing, that this were possible. "Alright, well,…I'm glad. I didn't know you were…currently occupied, Edmond. That's wonderful. Why don't you bring her over for supper soon? It'll be a good excuse to see your nephews. You haven't seen them in months, and they always ask for you."

"Leo, please," as Edmond attempted to quell this possibility.

"Please what…?"

"The only significance I am to them is a mustache, which they almost pull off every time I'm there."

"They *like* your mustache," Leopold couldn't help but smile at this.

"How underexposed to society are your children? They've never seen a mustache?"

"Apparently, not like *yours*."

"You should take them to a barber shop. I'm sure to them it would be like visiting the Louvre."

"They are children, Edmond."

"That's precisely my point."

"You were a child once. Remember?"

"I don't. That's the difference between us, Leopold. You remember because you still *are* a child. What's even more astonishing is that you *have* them."

"That's what men do."

Edmond was halted by this. "What the hell are you insinuating?"

"Nothing. My God, I'm not suggesting anything. You're most certainly a man. Just...a man without a wife and child. It's not against the law. Simply...odd."

As Edmond looked away, "Yes. Odd. And you're quite normal."

Leopold once again looked at the side of Edmond's face, before turning back to the window, as he watched the smoke emanating from a nearby factory chimney which soon faded into the sky. He had resigned that he would not attempt to initiate further discussion with Edmond for the duration of their trip, and yet, eventually, Edmond would:

"Do they know yet?" he asked without looking at Leo, emphasizing how confidential such a question needed to be. Of course, this would be one subject that Leopold would have preferred to avoid. "Not yet," he begrudgingly replied,

"You should tell them before they find out in other ways. They're getting older."

"Yes, I know," as Leopold continued to gaze out the window, trying to seek comfort in the trees and bales of hay he was now observing…

"It's better if they hear it from you. They'll be more prepared."

"They won't be doing this, Edmond, I assure you. It's enough that *I'm* doing it."

Slowly, Edmond turned to him, nearly offended. "It's your trade, Leopold."

"Well, it doesn't have to be my sons'. Just because they'll be men doesn't mean that they have to be fated into this."

"They don't have to be *fated* into it, but at least they have the option to choose."

"I don't want them to choose this, Edmond. Traditions can be created anew."

"And yet you want more money," as Edmond again turned away, his disappointment apparent, and yet it was not something unexpected, from Leo's view.

"I simply want them to feel that they can be…something else. God knows father never gave us such an option," Leopold nearly pleaded to Edmond, who remained silent.

He did always have a subtle need to please Edmond in some way, or at least to not dissatisfy him. This may have even been more pronounced since the sudden death of their father 15 years earlier, which ultimately elevated Edmond to Chief Executioner. But the reality of Leo's family life conjoined with his profession had become an increasingly visible source of stress for him. He had been in his line of work almost as long as Edmond, and was no longer a young man himself. What could a 42 year-old man abruptly start doing anew at such a life stage? These thoughts had appeared with increased regularity, and yet there was no one he could convey them to, aside from Michelle, without fearing judgment. Edmond would always be the most important opinion for him and yet he could not take comfort in it, for Edmond only knew one way of life. The pride he took in his profession appeared to take precedence over everything else. It was clear to Leopold that, just as Edmond seemed destined to live out his life as the executioner, so would he as his assistant. For the moment, it appeared the only thing that Leopold had control over was what his sons could one day become.

Again, they sat and listened to the engine and the scraping of the train wheels against the tracks, underscored by Claude. Despite this, Leo tried to suppress the mundane sounds with what was most joyful to him, which was usually speaking in some way of his sons, not surprisingly named after his favorite artists; Vincent (after Van Gogh) and Auguste, who would always be referred to as "Auggie" (after Auguste Rodin):

"Vincent's become quite the painter. You should see what he made for his art class; an oil of a flock of pigeons crapping over the Alps. Just beautiful."

"Yes, it sounds lovely," Edmond replied, clearly unimpressed.

"He's only 12 and already he has your gift for color, when you used to paint."

"I don't paint."

"I'm saying when you *used* to –"

"I don't paint, Leo."

Leopold looked at him, weakly snickered, then turned to the window defeatedly. "Father used to say it was a wasteful pursuit."

"It's a pastime. Not a trade. I agreed with him," Edmond replied, as if this were a mantra he had long repeated to himself.

"He said the same to me about my woodcarvings. Mother encouraged me, yet father… Well,…" Leo trailed off, realizing how superfluous his memories were. "Do you still have your easel?"

Edmond turned to him, "Leo, what are you doing?"

"What?"

"Why are we having such a discussion?"

"Why not? Must we always simply stare ahead and listen to Claude snore?"

"Frankly, I'd prefer it. Either follow Claude in his hibernation or say nothing, please."

Leopold took a moment. "I didn't say that I have no respect for what we do, Edmond."

"Then what are you saying?"

He felt he could not phrase his thoughts in any way that would make sense to Edmond. "Nothing," would be his only reply, as he returned to the passing buildings outside his window. Edmond looked at him, not oblivious to his musing. It would take him several moments, as they were now within minutes of entering Paris, to temper his resentment that Leo had inadvertently stoked and attempt to provide a semblance of encouragement to him:

"Leo, when I feel the time is appropriate, I'll speak to Ratier regarding your wages, alright? But until then, you need to reevaluate your mindset towards your profession. This is what you do. What you've *been* doing. If not this, what else is there for you?"

Leo did not appear to be much encouraged by this proposal, but indulged his brother. "You're right, Edmond. How foolish of me," he whispered, numbingly, as he continued looking out, but not seeing anything now but the bleakness of his future. "Thank you for…keeping my head on straight. So to speak."

Edmond looked at Leopold, resisting a reprimand, as Leo well knew of his brother's staunch objection to decapitation humor.

The remainder of their trip would be in silence.

***

3

~

Edmond's journal entry regarding the execution of Jean Paul Le Der would read as follows:

The 22ⁿᵈ of March, 1913 (Versailles). Jean Paul Le Der was executed as a result of eighteen counts of Assault and twelve counts of Thievery. As per his court testimony, his past appeared to have fated him into such a criminal existence, as the offspring of a prostitute mother and an absent father. For one can only assume that if his father were lascivious enough to embark on a sexual foray with such a woman of loose morals that it is quite likely that he engaged in various other sorts of depraved behavior, which would have been inevitable in his offspring. On the day of his execution, Le Der's eyes looked at me, briefly, and in them was no plea for life, but a certain resignation that his future, if permitted to live beyond this day, would render little in the way of merit. This may have been his wisest and most charitable thought.

***

Phillipe Du Jonet was a seasoned reporter with *The Paris Herald.* Just prior to his departure for Versailles, Edmond would be informed by Ratier that upon his return he was to grant an interview, which was assured to be a relatively brief and rudimentary article regarding the state of capital punishment in France. It still baffled Edmond just why he would be requested for such an interview, which in all his years, he had never been asked to grant before. Yes, he had established a bit of a clandestine reputation, perhaps, given his years of service, but it certainly didn't seem to warrant this responsibility. It would be more common for the Minister of Justice to speak publicly on such an issue. And if not he, then someone of a status and certainly a wage level far in excess of Edmond's. However, it would seem that, at least to higher-ranking representatives, this matter was trivial and of less importance, especially considering the problems Germany was rumored to be creating in much of Europe.

But it was a genuine aversion Edmond had as any sort of public personality, even for a brief, innocuous article, that most affected him, which took significant precedence over why he would be asked to speak with a journalist.

"I would like to have you standing, if it's all the same to you, monsieur," Du Jonet requested, as the photographer set up his camera several feet away.

"Standing?"

"Yes. Beside the chopper, if you'd be so kind."

"The what?" Edmond took a moment to absorb Du Jonet's terminology.

"I'm sorry. You know what I mean. The…"

"Guillotine," Edmond corrected.

"Yes. The guillotine, if you'd be so kind," Du Jonet smiled, seeming less apologetic than amused at his faux pas.

It was requested by Du Jonet that the guillotine be made available for their interview, which meant that their meeting would take place in the storage room of the Justice Department. Edmond, already ill at ease with being photographed, let alone alongside his notable device, tentatively moved beside it.

"May we have you place your foot in the…head whatnot?" barked the photographer, whose tact seemed germane to that of Du Jonet.

Again, Edmond was struck by the sheer lack of respect offered for the tool of his trade: "In the *'head whatnot'*?"

"Oh, that would be perfect. Yes, would you mind placing your foot in the head whatnot?" Du Jonet concurred.

"Gentlemen, it is called the *lunette*. And yes, I *would* mind," Edmond summoned, with restrained audacity.

"You would?" questioned Du Jonet.

"Yes, I would. With all due respect, I don't believe that I'm posing for a cigar box."

"Oh, well…it's just that it would make for a very distinguished image of you."

"I would deem it disrespectful to this device."

"Disrespectful, sir?"

"Yes. This is not a footstool. This is a carefully hand-crafted piece of equipment, and I do not wish to make light of it, particularly for public consumption."

"Yes, but –"

"Now, at the behest of Minister Ratier, you may ask me a few questions and take one or two photographs of me in a dignified light, but beyond that, I'm afraid I cannot indulge you, gentlemen." Edmond understood well enough that however dutiful he may have been to his superiors, it did not mean that his standards of his profession should soften. Whereas, from Du Jonet's perspective, Edmond was a unique and fascinating specimen before him. And while his effusive persona would be somewhat overbearing to Edmond, given his reserved nature, Du Jonet was willing to make every attempt to appease him.

"That's fine, sir. I can certainly respect that. How about we simply take one of you standing beside it. Would that be acceptable?"

"That would be fine," Edmond reluctantly conceded.

"Excellent!" as Du Jonet directed the photographer to make a slight adjustment, then returned his focus to Edmond. "And I'll just ask you a few questions."

"That's fine."

Edmond stood rigidly beside the guillotine…

"Now, Monsieur de Capitoir…"

The photographer took the first photo, as the brightness of the bulb and the sound of its detonation simultaneously blinded and jolted Edmond, "AHHH! Bloody hell…!!!"

"Monsieur, are you all right…?" as Du Jonet approached him.

"Are you going to take my photograph or throw explosives in my direction?!" as Edmond repeatedly blinked to restore his vision…

"That was merely the flashbulb, sir. I'm sure that you're familiar with that."

"Well,…my apologies, then. It's…been some time since I've had a photograph taken. I thought they'd made some advancements in that time," he said with some embarrassment.

"I'm afraid that's as advanced as we've become, thus far. Are you able to proceed?"

Edmond rubbed his eyes and continued blinking, before feeling comfortable enough to resume.

"Perhaps we can take one of him in more of a profile," the photographer suggested.

"Yes, yes! That might work," Du Jonet agreed. "Monsieur, perhaps you could look in my direction rather than directly into the camera's. I believe that may work a little better for you."

"Very well," Edmond begrudgingly consented, as he braced himself…

"Thank you," as Du Jonet aimed his pen at his writing pad again. "Now, Monsieur…"

The photographer took the second photo, as the brightness of the bulb and its detonation appeared to have the same effect: "OH, BLOODY HELL!!!" Edmond bellowed.

"That will do," smiled the photographer, oblivious to Edmond's state…

"Blinding your subject will do?!" as Edmond repeatedly blinked, while supporting himself against the guillotine's slats…

"Sir, that will be all the photographs we will subject you to, I assure you. Rafael, thank you."

As the Photographer swiftly gathered his equipment, Du Jonet gingerly approached Edmond again… "Are you all right, sir? Do you need a doctor?"

Edmond slowly established his vision, yet again. "No, just, please, give me a moment. I believe my retinas are moving back into place."

"Of course, sir." Du Jonet waited, as the photographer departed. He was now alone with Edmond. whom he had only heard about from afar: a man whose name was largely unknown to the public, but whose unassuming yet efficient work, not to mention his considerable number of beheadings, made him an object of particular intrigue for Du Jonet.

"All right, shall we get on with this, please?" Edmond asserted.

"Would you like to sit?"

"I'd prefer to stand. Thank you."

"Very well," as Du Jonet once again aimed his pen at his pad, then leaned into Edmond, as if about to hear a favorite ghost story: "Now, sir, please tell me a bit about your device."

"Well, of course, this isn't *my* creation. Simply one that I administer."

"Understood."

It took such a seemingly benign question to make Edmond speak with any authority, for, unbeknownst to Du Jonet, he did have a considerable admiration for the history of the instrument and certainly had not had occasion in many years to expound on its origins: "You see, the existence of the guillotine is certainly not new, as you may or may not know. One of the more interesting facts is that, where it is named after Dr. Joseph Guillotin, few are aware that he is not the actual inventor."

"Is that so?"

"Indeed. There isn't an official creator of the device that is known, however Antoine Louis was credited with its early development in the late 18th century, and then in 1872, Leon Berger made certain refinements which is what is currently utilized today. However, Guillotin *was* the principle advocate for decapitation as an efficient method of capital punishment, as he believed it proved the most dignified and the least painful."

"The *least* painful?" Du Jonet asked, with amused skepticism.

"Correct."

"Pardon me, sir, but how is one who is having their head severed undergoing less pain than one who is shot or hanged?"

With his usual professorial efficiency and emotional detachment, Edmond would explain: "It's instantaneous. There is no prolonged suffering, like many who have underwent other forms of execution."

"Can you expand upon this?"

"Well, for instance, when one is hanged, they, in many cases, can undergo a gradual, tortuous suffering; a snap of the neck is never a guarantee and, as a result, the victim may undergo a slow and arduous asphyxiation. Whereas one who is shot may not be done so in the anatomical areas which would prompt a quick demise, due to a less than accurate marksman. However, the guillotine does not waste time in achieving its goal. The condemned is dead instantly, as the blood transmittal to the brain is promptly severed, thus ceasing consciousness."

"Are you saying that the victim experiences *no* pain?"

"Virtually none," Edmond replied, with near ebullient pride.

"Well, with all due respect, monsieur, how would you know this for certain?" Du Jonet inquired, with an ironic smile.

"I beg your pardon?"

"Well, surely you haven't tried it yourself. Certainly no one has any first-hand knowledge that decapitation is virtually painless."

"Knowing the efficiency of this device, I can safely conclude that it is."

"Most interesting," as Du Jonet rapidly jotted...

"Yes, I suppose so. Will that be all, then?", as Edmond motioned to escort Du Jonet from the premises…

"Not quite, monsieur. If you would kindly tell me a bit about your recent performance."

Edmond absorbed this for a moment. "Performance?"

"Why, yes, I believe you were last –"

"Excuse me, monsieur. I may perform the service of execution, but that does not make the event a *'performance'* any more than a tooth extraction as performed by a dentist. You may call it a procedure but it most certainly is not to be construed as a sort of Vau de Vire."

Du Jonet was taken aback by Edmond's affrontery, and yet he was impressed by how committed Edmond was to his trade perhaps more than any other who had ever held his position. In his mind, his knowledge, while considerable, seemed to justify the intriguingly macabre nature of his profession.

Du Jonet corrected himself: "Noted, sir. So you would consider an apt term 'procedure' and yourself as…?

"A government servant."

"However, you would certainly agree that there is a degree of showmanship in what you do."

"I wouldn't at all."

"Well, it's just that you do attract a bit of an audience."

"I do not *attract* them, monsieur. The event attracts them, as I suppose it has throughout history, to some degree."

"And why do you suppose that is?"

"I can only assume it's because they feel that the act is justified."

Du Jonet noted this, with an expanding smile at the unique perspective he was obtaining, which was certainly rare in the scope of France's journalistic history.

"Very well, sir," as Du Jonet took a confident saunter to glean a better look at the device that Edmond clearly was protective of. "Now, you have held your post of Chief Executioner for how long now?"

"It will be 15 years, upon the 12th of December."

"That's longer than *most* have held your title, isn't it?"

"Longer than many, but not all."

"But as far as any previous one who has been responsible for administering all of France's executions, you would be second only to your father, correct?"

It was at this point that Edmond sensed that this harmless interview with Du Jonet had a motivation beyond the rudimentary. In truth, Edmond would not have ascended to his current position as young as he was if not for his father suffering a massive heart attack just days after his 50th birthday. He would collapse into Edmond's arms on the platform at Gare du Nord, on a return from an execution in Dijon.

"I suppose that is so, yes," he hesitantly revealed.

"And yet, in your near 15 years, you have already executed more than your father during the entirety of his time in the position you now hold, yes?"

"Well, I don't have the numbers in my head, but that may be true."

"Well, according to the documents that Minister Ratier has provided, that is *certainly* true," Du Jonet followed, as though savoring these statistics.

"Well, I… One such as myself certainly can't take credit for a growing crime rate…"

"But you are most expeditious. Perhaps the fastest ever by those who have born witness to your administrations."

Edmond's heart was beating slightly faster, but it was not the kind he experienced at Maison's Patisserie before the liquid blue eyes of a woman whose name he still did not know. This was one of unsettlement. A rare feeling, for certain, that could only come with a sense of obligation to unearth what he never fathomed would be broached in such a forum. And now he was even being asked to reveal the inner machinations of his duties, which he long deemed sacred.

"I've…always felt that there is no need to prolong the inevitable."

"Do you feel that your victims appreciate such a courtesy?"

"The condemned are not *my* victims," Edmond again corrected. "They are the perpetrators of their own heinous acts. Monsieur Du Jonet, are we almost finished here — ?"

"Just a few more questions, monsieur."

"Well, I really must — "

"What would you say are the essentials that would lead to one's…success in your field?"

What sort of a foolish question is that? Edmond thought. It dawned on him, at this point, that he could simply end this interview, for it had clearly become something that he hadn't been prepared for nor agreed to. But, at the same time, he felt imprisoned now by the obligation he had to the Justice Department. To his country. To Ratier. For him to suddenly cease the interview would undoubtedly serve to represent capital punishment in an inaccurate light. As these thoughts crossed his mind, he barely managed to recall the question: "The essentials are…proper training."

"Indeed. It would seem. And you were trained by your father, yes?"

"Yes, I…I was his assistant."

"And he was trained by *his* father?"

"Yes, but, monsieur, I think that we've — "

"So would it be fair to say that a sort of nepotism is necessary?" Du Jonet appeared to be almost half-jesting with this inquiry. Little would he know that Edmond never embraced the notion of simply falling into a profession by way of bloodline. In truth, it offended him:

"Monsieur, just because one is related to another does not in and of itself mean that one will inherently possess the skills to succeed at this position. Aside from proper training, efficiency is a definite and necessary attribute."

"Efficiency," Du Jonet jotted…

"Yes. And economy of time," Edmond fired.

"Economy of time," Du Jonet jotted…

"Yes."

"And a strong stomach?" Du Jonet halted his writing, and smiled at Edmond, which seemed on the verge of an outright guffaw.

At this, Edmond merely gazed at him, now hardly able to contain his resentment and his sense of feeling used for something beyond his expectancy. Du Jonet managed to contain himself, and, for the moment, appeared almost affectively embarrassed by his attempted jest.

"My apologies, sir. I was simply trying to add a bit of levity, considering."

"Levity at my expense is not appreciated, Monsieur Du Jonet."

"I understand. Again, my apologies."

Edmond took a moment to accept this. "Very well. Now, if there will be nothing else — "

"Actually, sir, if I may, I'd be curious to know how you manage to remove yourself."

"I don't *remove* myself, monsieur. Otherwise, who would pull the lever?"

Edmond's sarcasm was usually dormant, with the exception of his occasional responses to Leopold. But, to his surprise, it had surfaced in his impatience with how this interview was proceeding – or, rather, lingering.

"Yes, well…" Du Jonet faintly smiled, then resumed: "In any event, it is said that you attend the sentencing of many of the condemned, prior to them being brought unto your authority."

How would he know this? Edmond mused. It quickly dawned on him that, of course, journalists often attended sentencings and court proceedings. But even judges did not seem to be aware of Edmond's presence, since it was never an official obligation, nor did Edmond seek to make his presence known. By contrast, he would sit in the back of a court room and, amidst the other attendees and officials, more often felt blended with the walls, before discreetly departing.

With increased reluctance, he divulged, "With time permitting, as often as I can."

"Is that a requirement of your position?"

"No, but I require it of myself.

"I'm curious to know if your father did the same?"

Why on earth does he care? Edmond thought. "I don't recall him doing so, no."

"Might I ask why *you* do?"

"I simply feel that, as a servant of the government, I should give as much of myself as possible to the inner workings of our great justice system."

"Out of curiosity?"

"Out of respect."

"And for the condemned?"

"What about them?"

"Do you respect them?"

"Might I ask why you would care, monsieur?"

Du Jonet smiled, "Pure journalistic curiosity. Nothing more. One would think, or at least *I* would, that you have some sympathy, considering how briskly you work."

"Well, I certainly don't *respect* whatever acts they've committed that would bring them before me. However, I do feel a certain responsibility to not extend their punishment. And that is as much as I would care to divulge…"

"And to what would you attribute your apparent immunity?"

"I beg your pardon."

"Well, I would think that the most essential requirement of the man responsible for all of France's executions would be a certain resiliency towards, what most would consider to be,…quite a repellent profession."

"Perhaps you should ask those who are repelled. Are they repelled at what I'm doing? Or do they feel it is strongly justified in light of the fact that these criminals have committed atrocities which, in fact, *are* repellent?"

"That's…an interesting question."

"Yes, isn't it. Now, monsieur, if you don't mind…"

"And so you don't suppose that your resiliency has *anything* to do with the de Capitoir blood?"

Edmond's motion to escort Du Jonet from the premises was halted by this. He now clearly deduced that Du Jonet's interests had little to do with a profession that, up until now, had largely been unreported in much detail, nor was this about criminal statistics. Where his interests seemed to reside were in what sort of mind Edmond had. What sort of man could do this, and for such a considerable length of time. It seemed to be a psychological probing that Du Jonet was after, which, finally, resulted in Edmond's inability to conceal a feeling of betrayal.

He gazed at Du Jonet, "I see journalists have their *own* guillotine."

Du Jonet was struck by this, as though finally absorbing an answer that Edmond provided, "I'm sorry, monsieur…?"

"Is the point of this interview to make me out to be some mythical creature from the Middle Ages, to whom you are the first to probe?"

"Monsieur, my apologies, but it *is* the nature of my trade to report –"

"If cunning and duplicity are the *nature* of your trade, then perhaps you should look into another line of work."

"Monsieur, it's simply that I believe that the public may have a certain…curiosity."

"With what?"

"Well,…with *you*," Du Jonet grinned, as if this would be a pleasant bit of news.

Why on earth would they be curious of me? Edmond unfathomably wondered, before gaining a firmer stance to speak: "Monsieur, I live my life with a certain anonymity which I wish to continue. As long as my government respects me and my work, that is all that I require. *I certainly don't require this!"*

With that, Edmond directed his open hand to the entrance, which would clearly symbolize to Du Jonet that he was bringing this reportorial exchange to an end. Du Jonet would simply nod politely, before departing. And yet this was hardly a victory for Edmond, for it seemed that this journalist obtained more information from this heretofore nameless representative of death than anyone else could fathom. And to Edmond's further unsettlement, what he would use of this information would be unknown and unattainable to him,…until the article appeared in print.

***

4

~

Several days later, Edmond would take his usual, unassuming stroll to the Justice Department from his modest apartment building in Saint-Fargeau. Walks throughout much of Paris were a pleasure of his, as he admired the architecture, the craftsmanship of the many facades, the gothic structures that loomed over streets as if they erupted from the earth. More often than not, he felt pleasantly invisible in these excursions, as he generally did when he elected to treat himself to a Moliere revival or a favorite opera or museum exhibit. It was early morning, but the cobblestones still reverberated from nearby horse carriages and occasional cars. Various smells were always particularly strong at the onset of a Parisian day: baked bread from miniscule cafes, freshly caught fish being transported by the mongers, who were no less odiferous. These conflicting smells, however, merely underscored a certain peace that Edmond usually could enjoy in these moments.

"Monsieur!" a distant female voice called, with even a similar cadence to that of the young woman from Maison's. *Could it be her?* "Monsieur de Capitoir!" the same voice followed. Edmond did not recall ever disclosing his name to Juliette, nor did he know hers for that matter. But it would nevertheless be a pleasant surprise to see her. As Edmond turned, he was stunned to discover a woman rushing towards him whom he had never seen before. What was even more absurd was that she appeared to be followed by at least two other women, and even several men, all of ages ranging from thirties to Edmond's own. *What on earth...?* Edmond clutched his briefcase to his chest along with his cane, as they quickly encircled him:

"Monsieur de Capitoir!"

"We just want to say that we greatly admire your work!"

"Your professionalism!"

"The authority by which you pull that lever!"

"It's quite a service, indeed, sir."

"Well, I'm...I really..." Edmond could only stammer at this assault...

"Is it true that you can remove one's head faster than you can say *guillotine*?"

"I beg your – ?"

"In this newspaper article, you claimed that that was true," a young man jutted his hand out at Edmond, which, within his chapped and ink-blackened fingers, contained the cover page of the *Paris Herald*'s latest edition.

"In this...?" Edmond stopped to look at the front-page article quickly enough to gander at one sentence – "*While he may possess a reserved nature, Chief Executioner de Capitoir can hardly contain his grandiloquence when speaking of his own efficiency –*

to the extent that his procedures have been known to elapse before one can utter 'guillotine'."

Edmond could barely form words, "I...I never said any such thing."

"Oh, modesty will get you everywhere, monsieur," said a strangely flirtatious auburn-haired woman, who attempted to sidle next to Edmond through the effusive circle of admirers...

"Would you mind at least saying *guillotine* once for us?"

"I'd find it quite intoxicating."

"Please, madame, get a hold of yourself..." as Edmond was now shaking, both due to the small wave of strangers around him as well as from the newly received knowledge that whatever Du Jonet elected to publish was, judging by these results, nothing of remote benefit to him. By contrast, Edmond knew well enough, without even reading the article in full, that if it could render such a violation of his privacy, it certainly would not bode well for his profession.

"May I have an autograph?" asked another young woman, who appeared conjoined with an older sister...

"A what?" Edmond gasped.

"Me as well, please? I'd be ever appreciative, sir..." asked another ambient voice, as the faces blended into one amorphous beast before Edmond's eyes...

As another hand clasping a paper punched through forcefully amidst the other violently jutting hands and harsh cacophony of autograph requests, a nearly euphoric shriek would rise above all: "Make mine *'To Patrice – Keep your head on your shoulders!- Love, Monsieur de Capitoir'!!!"*

***

After Edmond fled from the throng that nearly engulfed him, he managed to discreetly purchase a copy of *The Paris Herald*, before looking for a nearby alley in which to read Du Jonet's article without distraction. Before he went in, he waited for a mother to pass on the sidewalk with her young son. While the mother only appeared focused on their destination, her young boy's bulging eyes stared at Edmond, as he was being swiftly tugged along. Edmond looked at this child, not out of his usual distaste for children, but out of a deeper concern: *Who is he looking at?* Edmond mused, as the boy continued staring until the mother and he turned the next corner. Momentarily, Edmond saw something else in the young lad; an innocence that seemed strangely familiar, if equally unsettling. He gazed at the very corner that they faded from, before urgently ducking into a particularly filthy alley way, his heart rapidly beating, before his eyes came upon it:

"To be face to face with a man who has not only seen death within arm's length, but has been responsible for it, can be unsettling for most to fathom. I speak not of a criminal, of course, as the criminals, ironically, are his victims. I speak of France's Chief Executioner, one Edmond de Capitoir: not merely a servant to his government, as he'd preferred to be considered, but a man whose top hat and gallic

mustache have, for some years now, given him the distinction of a well-attired grim reaper. And while this journalist can assure you that Monsieur de Capitoir is very much made of the skin, bones and blood that makes up all human beings, one can't help but wonder from where his immunity derives. One can further not help but attribute it to genetics, for this position has managed to become a family trade since the mid-1800s, wherein Mr. de Capitoir's own grandfather held the post. Men in this field have, admittedly, wallowed in a preferred anonymity. 'Who would want to speak with such an individual?', one may ask. And yet one cannot help but wonder what prompts citizens of 20th Century France to still attend these gratuitous exhibitions, let alone anywhere else in Europe. Is it a sense of justice, as de Capitoir wishes to claim? Or is it a fascination that, however morbid, has heretofore gone unspoken among civil circles?"

Edmond read on, then uneasily stared out at the amassing pedestrians and horse carriages populating the streets. He was now nearly afraid to exit out of the alley, despite the rotting stench emanating from the adjacent waste cans. He had always felt confidently enough, and perhaps without even giving it much thought, that his life would continue on with a cherished anonymity that largely accompanied the lives of his father and grandfather. Given his inherent shyness, it always seemed that that would be one of the chief attributes of his profession. He never judged how others outside of the Justice Department would feel about his trade of choice, but also disclosed it to no one. If neighbors somehow found out, they would never be so bold as to broach it with him, for chances were likely that they had never exchanged many words with Edmond prior, if at all. Yet now, it felt as if he was unlawfully unveiled. The curtain was slightly open, and could now be looked into by the masses. *How many will read this?* Edmond wondered, as he continued to quickly glance at the many faces that passed by. It was a daily paper, after all. Considering the murmurings of France's involvement in a possible war with Germany, it would seem probable that such an invasive expose′ would quickly fade in its cultural importance.

But what if it doesn't? Edmond asked himself.

***

"*Monsieur de Capitoir?*" Edmond asked almost pleadingly, as Ratier bit into a particularly runny quail egg which was draped over the heel of a baguette, then swallowed…

"Well, that's your name, is it not, Edmond?" smiled a befuddled Ratier.

"But, sir, no one has ever addressed me as such on the street. Why, they haven't addressed me at *all*, frankly."

"Well, now some may. There's certainly nothing wrong with that, is there?"

"Well, sir, it's just…not something to which I'm accustomed."

"That may well be, Edmond, and I can appreciate that, however, you've always known that your very position is representative. You can't have assumed that you would always be anonymous. Why, to these citizens, you symbolize something."

"And what is that?"

"You symbolize discipline. Professionalism," then with a pleasant if apparent reluctance, he would add: "And, perhaps, other elements as well."

"What…other elements, sir?

"Well, fear."

"Fear?"

"Well, of course, Edmond. My God, you're chopping heads, not tomatoes."

Edmond absorbed Ratier's last sentence, and, as he would only do in his superior's company, would suppress his displeasure at his callus phrasing. "I'm aware of my profession, sir. I just… *Fear?* What kind of an impression is that?"

Ratier nearly laughed, but contained himself for the moment. In the three years in which he'd held the title of Minister of Justice, he had never seen Edmond appear even the slightest bit unsettled. By contrast, Edmond's staunch predictability was always something that Ratier could rely upon. Even if he might've preferred a more personable man in the role of Chief Executioner, his trust in Edmond was, in the end, a comfort – if a rather bland one. However, the Edmond he saw before him now was more of an anomaly – as it simply struck him as odd that he, even a relatively introverted man, could be so unnerved when, perhaps, Ratier felt that he should be embracing a momentary notoriety, regardless of its impetus.

"It's ideal, Edmond. People are attracted to their fears, and yet remain fearful. The public is aware that there is price to be paid for those who violate France's laws. And to them, you represent the law."

"True, but, with all due respect, Minister, police and lawyers *also* represent the law."

Ratier took in this observation, before wiping some residual yolk from the corners of his mouth. "Well, yes, they do, but...in a different, less mythical way, if you will. But, Edmond, *you* actually carry out everyone's greatest curiosity."

"But...why are they suddenly curious?"

"Edmond, they've *always* been," Ratier continued, still surprised by Edmond's ignorance on this subject. "Perhaps you've been unaware of this until now but, to many in France, the executioner has remained an intriguingly ambiguous figure. Many have not really believed the guillotine still existed in modern day France until witnessing an execution firsthand. And when they have, it's...well, I suppose it's as if a novel has come to life before them. Then it becomes a source of discussion in small circles,...which ultimately grow. And that's basically what's happened with you, particularly due to your outstanding productivity and longevity in the position."

"I appreciate that, sir, but I just don't feel that it's proper that my role is upstaging our justice system."

"Edmond, it's certainly not."

"With all due respect, Minister, I feel that it is."

"Well, if it is, I can assure you that no one is objecting."

"But, sir, I'm…I just don't know if I can handle such attention."

"Edmond, if you've managed thus far, what difference will a small, insignificant newspaper article make?"

"But, sir, it is as a result of this very article that I was accosted in the street by fanatics."

"How many government officials can say *that*?" Ratier grinned.

"Minister, for much of my tenure, I have enjoyed a certain obscurity."

"Yes, Edmond, I'm aware. And I'm certain that very little will change."

"But it *has* changed. I was never approached before, and now I'm afraid it may happen with disturbing frequency. I always thought that my work would speak enough."

"It speaks handsomely. My Lord, you're a wizard with the chopper, Edmond. I'm simply pointing out that, on occasion, you may be asked to speak with your mouth and not solely with the blade."

"Speak to whom?"

"To *anybody*, Edmond. You are representing your country, remember?"

"Yes, sir. I know."

"Why that's why we had you give the interview in the first place, as a respected representative of your government."

"That was certainly my intention, sir."

"Of course."

"And yet, sir, it seems as if Du Jonet has taken license with certain facts which, I feel, may distort people's perception."

"Perception of what?"

"Well, of *me*, sir. An article which I thought was simply intended to profile the current role of capital punishment in France has, instead, become a rather invasive profile of myself."

"Edmond, let me speak to you frankly," as he tossed down his napkin alongside his nearly emptied plate. "The timing of this article was not intended as arbitrary."

"What do you mean, sir?"

"Well, you're aware that crime has been mounting throughout many areas of France."

"Yes, sir."

"Therefore, what we hoped this article would do is assist in the diminishment of criminal acts, and we think it will. Now, yes, perhaps Du Jonet went off on a bit of tangent so, as a result, this may be at the expense of you dealing with the occasional autograph seeker who may deem you as more approachable now, but I can assure you, Edmond, that it will only be a temporary fascination. What ultimately will be achieved is an increased awareness of the most severe repercussions of criminal behavior. Why, I'm certain that in a very short time you will be old news and your anonymity will resume. And you can happily continue on with your duties, unimpeded by any outside element, aside from your lovely family."

"I don't…I don't have a family, sir," Edmond reminded him, yet again.

"Really?"

"Yes, sir."

"Are you certain?"

"Quite, sir."

"None?"

"Not…of my own, sir."

"Why, I could have sworn that you were married."

"No, sir."

"Have you ever been?"

"Never, sir."

"Really."

"Truly, sir."

Ratier thought to himself for a moment, before a smile came to him: "Well,…perhaps this will be what entices a certain female to your door, Edmond. A little celebrity status never hurt anybody."

Edmond remained before Ratier, as the forced grin, reminiscent of a hammock supported by two weakening trees, returned to his face…

***

5

~

The ensuing weeks saw Edmond and his two-man crew of Leopold and Claude perform administrations in their home city of Paris, followed by Lyon, and then a return to Versailles. Each administration was rendered with the usual unspoken efficiency that had long been the standard set by Edmond. The victims, respectively; Cecil Renot, Albert Jouvét and, in Versailles, Marcel Riemé, were administrations unaltered from any that had come previous, with only the slightest behavioral differences.

Renot, a convicted serial rapist of at least 11 women of varying age, stared ahead, as he waited to be placed along the bascule by Leo and Claude. Not unlike Jean Paul Le Der and others who had come before, there was a certain resignation that his demise was preferred to him over a continued life. Whereas Jouvét, who had killed his father in a rage over his refusal to grant him a sizable loan, was more unsettled. This was often the difference that Edmond witnessed in these victims. A seasoned criminal would often be stoic or, at times, even apathetic to his fate. Edmond often felt, without hearing discernible proof, that such criminals saw little option that was better for them. If they were allowed to live and, ultimately, be freed, they would undoubtedly commit such crimes again. If they were sentenced to a lengthy imprisonment, they would simply go insane. But if it were a single act, one that could be attributed to a crime of passion, then it was often expected that the assailant would wear their regret and paralyzed fear like a veritable mask. Such was the case with Jouvét, who sobbed incessantly. Even as Leopold awkwardly placed the sack over his head, he could still see the tears streaming down his neck, as if a waterfall.

These particular types of administrations would remind Leo all the more that these were undoubtedly human beings, regardless of their crimes, who were being put to death. Jouvét's audible sobs, underscored by the nearby priest's rote prayer recitation, would soon make the silence all the more distinct once the blade dropped – followed only by gasps of the local townspeople.

It was here that Edmond, for the first time, took note of the amassed audience, for the gasps appeared much louder than he had noticed in the past.

In Versailles, Marcel Riemé, a career thief and forger, would follow the more traditional behavior of seasoned criminals prior to his ultimate demise, but the audience proved the contrary – as the swift gust of the descending blade through Rieme's neck was followed by a seeming wave of repulsed sound, followed by several distant regurgitations. This time, as Edmond, Leopold and Claude glanced around them, it was even more apparent that the crowds were becoming unquestionably larger.

***

As Leopold and Claude transported the guillotine to Gare de Versailles, Edmond would once again be obliged to obtain the favorite treats of Minister Ratier from Maison's. What might've normally become a tedious task that had no relation to his work was submerged by Edmond's desire to see the woman who worked there. On his short carriage ride there, he would occasionally notice eyes upon him. Whereas, in the past, there was always a glance or two that he witnessed that may've been attributed to nothing more than curiosity; now he was becoming unsettled – for he could not distinguish between casual glances and something more invasive. He would still prefer mere looks over anyone actually approaching him. Fortunately, they weren't nearly as aggressive as the group who accosted him in Paris on the morning Du Jonet's story appeared, but there were now a few who would linger after an execution, who appeared to wait for Edmond as if a chanteur after a performance. One or two approached him in Lyon, a few in Paris and several in Versailles, but none were forward enough to voice a particular request. They simply watched him depart from the prison, as if wanting to speak with him, but there was still a tenuousness. They looked as if he were a carnival animal that was trained enough to perform but could be unpredictable in any other circumstances. *But what compels them to even get that close?* Edmond mused on the ride to Maison's. *Well, at least that's as brazen as they've been. Let them fear me, as long as they don't ask anything of me.*

He still held hope that, with time, so would fade any residual effects of that article.

He stood outside the window of Maison's, crouching just out of sight. He looked in to see her, looking as she always did. So pure and undaunted. He watched her hand a small box to a young couple in their approximate twenties, as they bid her adieu before departing. Edmond now needed to be mindful of his surroundings. Who would know him? Who could've read that article? Who could've even attended the execution that morning, or in the recent past enough to recognize him?

He was already combatting a shyness when speaking with Juliette, but now, combined with having to shortly meet Leo and Claude at the nearby metro station, his confidence was even more challenged by elements he felt he could not control.

He entered, igniting the bell. She had just prior gone into the kitchen, which gave him an additional moment to gather himself. The smell upon entering had an almost medicinal effect on him. Not simply that it was a delectable scent, a blend of warm sweetness that was, otherwise, indescribable. It was that it represented how close she now was to him, despite the occasional metal tray clangs and faint sporadic growls from Maison in the kitchen. As he looked around, bathing in the aroma, he almost considered this a sort of heaven, though he'd come to no longer believe in one in any religious sense. He even felt safe, as if patrons could not enter while he was there; and the earliness of the morning had more often than not supported this possibility in the past.

She then entered behind the counter with a tray of elegant and perfectly aligned pastries, with what appeared to be a slight dollop of strawberry icing. As Edmond turned to discover her, her eyes met his: "Oh, good morning, monsieur," she said, with a certain recognition.

"Yes, and a good morning to you, madame," Edmond managed, through a sudden palpitation. She placed the trays to the side, then quickly wiped any residual powdered sugar from her hands. Edmond observed the tray, "Those look very decorative."

Juliette smiled, as she looked at them as well. "My father always says that presentation is nine-tenths of the law."

Edmond took a moment to absorb this. "Well, as legal as they are, I'm certain that they are equally sinful."

"They're made with rum. Would you like to try one? At no charge, of course."

"Oh, no, but thank you. The rum may alter my perception a bit, as I have a bit of a journey ahead."

"Saint Fargeau, yes?"

"I…well, yes. Yes, indeed," he blushed, taken aback by her memory. Even though it had only been weeks since his last visit, he still never dared assume that she would recall him.

"I didn't think that you'd be back so soon."

"Yes, well,…I…wasn't quite certain myself."

They shared a smile which, as it had before, was on the verge of becoming awkward in its silence. Edmond summoned, "How…how has business been for you, of late?"

"Oh, my father complains, but that's just his nature."

"I see."

"I would say that we're doing within our means."

"Well, I don't know the numbers but, from my view, he should be quite proud."

"That's very sweet of you to say."

"Well, it's not intended as mere flattery, I assure you. Men such as your father are the spine which keep France a civil and functioning country. There should be more like him."

"Yes, well,…I know *only* like him."

"Well, then…you live in a charmed world," Edmond followed. In his estimation, her response was further evidence of a lack of exposure to the outside world as he knew it.   He both envied this and was troubled by it.

"I'm so sorry. I don't believe I've taken your order, have I," she said with genuine surprise.

"Oh, well,…it's certainly through no fault of yours."

"It's just that I know you're pressed for time. The next train leaves shortly."

"Yes, well, thank you for…being attentive to that," he said with appreciation while, at the same time, he was reminded of the brevity of their time together. He flipped through his note pad, "Um…yes, I will have 12 of your famous éclairs…and 6 lemon custard tarts, please."

"Very well."

Not unlike Edmond's prior visit, he would take advantage of Juliette's distraction to, again, saunter towards the window and gander at the day, in pursuit of words: "It appears as if more precipitation is on its way, yes?"

As Juliette placed the lemon tarts in their own box, "Yes, it looks that way, doesn't it."

"Yes, it seems inevitable." He looked back at her, as she ducked behind the display case to obtain another tart, before he looked back out at the few passing pedestrians. "Hopefully, by the time you leave for the day, it will've subsided."

"Well, we only live upstairs, my father and I."

"Oh. I see," said Edmond, strangely reassured.

"However, God's tears are nothing to fear, as my mother used to say."

Edmond looked away from the monotony of the streets, and turned to Juliette. "Did she really say that?"

Juliette stopped for a moment, and smiled at how this appeared as a unique phrase to him. "Have you never heard that?"

"No, I'm afraid not."

"Of course, my father espouses the Socratic theory," she snickered.

"Yes, well… There is something to be said for science, yes?"

"*Some*thing, perhaps," she smiled again, as Edmond attempted the same, despite his feelings that anything that could be credited to God was difficult to take seriously.

As she resumed assembling the tarts in their box, Edmond sauntered back to the window, noticing that the traffic of the new day was somewhat increasing. He considered his next question carefully:

"Have you read the newspaper recently?"

He felt a pause in her, as her eyes peered over the counter, as she was still bent. "Was there an article about that?"

He swallowed, "About what?"

"I thought it might be in reference to something that we were talking about."

"Oh. You mean the weather?"

"Or Socrates," she giggled.

"Hah. Yes, yes. No, actually, I…I didn't read anything myself. I was simply curious if *you* had."

"No, I'm afraid I don't read the newspaper."

"Really," he exhaled.

"Really," as she slowly rose, curious of his line of questioning.

"So…you don't feel the need to be more informed of world events?"

"Why?"

"Well,…I don't know."

She smiled at him, cognizant that Edmond's reply well enough answered her question. She moved on to the eclairs, placing them in their own box, as Edmond again summoned: "Your father?"

"Yes?" she stopped, again peering over the counter in her crouched pose.

"Does he…read the paper?"

"Oh, dear, there's no time for that. It's all work. Time for a pipe and little else with him."

"I see."

As she resumed, before, again, Edmond summoned, "And your mother?"

There was a silence, as Juliette rose from behind the counter, and smiled as if not wanting to impose embarrassment on him. "She's passed on. For some years now."

He absorbed this. "My apologies," he whispered.

"For what?"

"Well, for…for losing her," he grasped, never having been an expert at condolences.

"I didn't lose her," she said with an unusual assurance. "I know where she is."

Edmond took this in, unable to find the words in which to respond. He knew she likely meant heaven. A place that he had grown to not merely question, but to outright disbelieve in. Perhaps his trade was a significant factor in this, but Edmond simply did not give it credence – and it was easy enough for it to never come up. Leo still considered himself a practicing Catholic, no doubt aided by his wife Michelle, particularly as a stabilizing source in the rearing of their two boys. But the growing limits of his and Leo's personal association did well to keep such religious discussions at bay. The clergymen who were often in attendance to grant final prayers were, in Edmond's estimation, a false comfort, but one that the victims were entitled to, not unlike the use of an anesthesia. To Edmond, it was more designed to alleviate pain, even if they may've secretly hoped for the summoning of angels.

He pressed on, almost despite himself: "Do you….do you have siblings?"

She stopped again, growing increasingly curious. "No. Just myself."

"Friends?"

She no longer could help but chuckle at his mounting curiosity. "I'm sorry. What about them?"

"Well, just… I assume someone who is as pleasant as yourself must have them, yes?"

Her smile remained, even as her suspicion was apparent. "Why do you ask?"

At this, Edmond could only admit to the absurdity of his inquisitiveness, to the extent where he would ask her about the entirety of her familial and social status after three years of his sporadic patronage. "That was a very silly question of me to pose."

"That's fine. You're just making conversation."

"And very poorly, at that. Please, my apologies."

Perhaps with anyone else, she may have simply continued with her work, but she felt compelled to answer, even if her answer was not one that could be considered boastful:

"Well, I work much of the time, and I like to read," she stopped, looked down at the counter, as her shyness was now giving way. "I suppose that I've chosen to be unto myself, more often than not."

"I see," he took this in, in a sort of humbled appreciation.

"Whereas I'm sure that *you* have a…considerable social circle."

"Why…why would you say that?"

"Well, I mean…I would think that just your travels alone would prompt you to meet…many interesting people, yes?"

"Well, I…yes. Of…of…of course." Edmond could hardly feign a further response to this, especially being that he would feel compelled to fabricate beyond his inherent abilities. To his surprise, Juliette did not appear eager to resume with placing the eclairs in their respective box, but looked somewhat compelled to speak further on this matter:

"I'm afraid I don't converse at much length with patrons either. Usually, people know exactly what they want and invite little else, and I've never been one to impose."

"I see," he smiled.

"Sometimes I even begin to chat with the pies just to stimulate my brain."

"Is that so?"

"I'm embarrassed to say."

"No, it's not embarrassing at all. I'm intrigued," and indeed he was.

"Well,…"

"What do they say?"

"They?" she asked, with surprise.

"Yes."

"The pies?"

"Yes."

"Well,…they   don't,   of   course. They're…pies," she said, delicately.

Edmond took a moment to realize the inanity of his question. "Yes, well…they are at that, aren't they," as his face quickly reddened.

"Oh, please, don't be embarrassed. Actually, considering how silly I was to mention it, your question made perfect sense," she smiled, and in so doing it would procure a smile from Edmond. "You're very witty," she followed.

Edmond took this in, never having heard such an observation directed at himself. "You're simply indulgent of my shortcomings."

"Just because I speak to a pastry on occasion doesn't mean that I'm easily humored."

They remained looking at each other for the moment, before Juliette abruptly broke out in laughter…

"Oh, dear, did… I'm sorry, did I – ?" Edmond felt compelled to apologize for the unknown…

"No, no. I was just thinking of something that you said the last time you were here."

"Something *I* said?" he asked, unfathomably.

"About your doctor prescribing pastries."

"Did I say such a thing?"

"Well, I suppose you have many retorts to recall, but, yes, that was one. Very ironic humor."

"How is that?"

"Well,…due to your aversion, of course."

He took a moment. "Yes. Yes, you…you remember that, as well," he said, nearly breathless.

Again, their eyes remained, without words said. For the moment, time was frozen.

"I…I put the tarts in a separate box," she said, softly, as she slowly slid the boxes towards him.

"Oh, that's… Thank – " The bell from the entrance door abruptly rang, at the same time that a loud clang of several trays were heard crashing to the kitchen floor - *"Damnit to hell!"* roared from the unseen Maison. Edmond tried to contain himself from the sudden assault of sounds...

"I'm sorry, one moment," she said softly, then to the entering patron: "I'll be right with you, monsieur."

"Very well. Thank you," the man replied, seemingly in a hurry. Juliette exited into the kitchen, while Edmond remained fairly rigid to the burly and bearded patron now standing closely behind him.

"Dear, I hope he didn't spill something delectable," the man remarked.

"Yes, let's…let's hope not," Edmond replied with reluctance, as he remained looking ahead.

"Well, there's more where that came from, I'm certain. This patisserie is a nearly bottomless well of sumptuous delights."

"Yes,…so…so I've heard," Edmond followed, hoping the man's commentary would quickly cease.

"My Lord, their Crème souffle..."

"Yes."

"Palmiers…"

"Yes, yes. Most delightful," Edmond managed, in a tone that now clearly requested that the man stop speaking.

This brought with it a sudden silence, as Edmond slightly turned his head to see if the man was still close behind, somehow hoping he had vanished. But this would be a mistake.

"You look rather familiar, sir. Have we met?"

"I'm afraid not, monsieur," Edmond replied, tersely.

"Well, with all due respect, you're not even looking at me, sir."

Edmond squeezed his cane handle anxiously, as he remained gazing at the back of the cash register. "I have a strong sense when I've met someone, sir. Trust me, we have not met."

"Well,…alright. I'm sorry to disturb you. It's just that…I rarely have had such a strong feeling that I've met or seen a person before, and yet been wrong."

"Yes, well…if we were always correct, our existence wouldn't be very compelling, would it."

"Yes, I…I suppose."

The man realized that he could not get a complete look at Edmond unless he were brazen enough to step in front of him in the line, but then noticed that he could see Edmond's face clearly in the mirrored signage that resided behind the counter. Juliette rushed out from the kitchen, "My apologies. Will there be – ?"

"My God!" involuntarily emanated from the man, as Edmond quickly took notice of his aghast expression in the mirror.

"Sir, are you alright?" Juliette asked.

Edmond remained still, but kept his stern focus on Juliette, "How much do I owe you, mada – ?"

"Ec..ec…excuse me," the man managed, before rushing out of the store.

Edmond struggled to ignore the patron's reaction, "I'm sorry, how much does that come to, madame?"

"Did you see that?"

"I'm sorry. See what?" Edmond feigned.

"That man. He looked at you and ran out like a scared cat."

"Ah, yes. I'm not surprised. He was behaving rather strangely," Edmond managed, digging deeply and, albeit quickly, into a reserve of vivid fabrication rarely used.

"Was he?"

"Oh, yes. I believe he was claiming to be Napoleon Bonaparte himself."

"No."

"Yes, I…I even recall him speaking in tongues near the metro station, at one point."

"Are you serious?"

"Does he come here often?"

"I believe he's been here a few times before, but…"

"Well, please be careful."

"Well, he's always seemed…"

"Sane?"

"Yes."

"Yes, well, a psychiatrist once said that sanity is merely a symptom of *in*sanity."

And with that, Juliette's surprise seemed to fade into a knowing grin: "This sounds a bit like your doctor who prescribed pastries."

Edmond could not help but be eased by her humor, even if he was unsettled at how far her curiosity would go. "Does it?"

"It does."

"Well,…perhaps they're colleagues," Edmond smiled. "Is…is your father all right?"

"Oh, yes. Hot tray. Not the first time," her expression gave clear evidence that this was true, and made it even more apparent that, without Edmond having officially met her father, Juliette was likely the only person who had the proper acumen to deal with his eccentricities and sporadic volatility.

And then it came, the most unexpected of inquiries: "May…may I ask your name?" she asked, with a certain reticence.

But, of course, Edmond dared not assume it was for anything unrelated to business, even though she had never asked prior. "Do…do you need that for the receipt?"

"No. Just…for myself."

"Oh. I see. Well, it's…it's Edmond," he replied, nearly breathless again.

"Nice to…officially meet you, Edmond."

"And…and yours is…?"

"Juliette," as the distant train whistle underscored it.

"Juliette," Edmond repeated through a smile, anxious, as he knew the whistle was the ultimate sign of their time, again, coming to an end…

***

6

~

"We almost missed the train," Leo exclaimed under a whisper, sitting alongside Edmond.

"Well, we didn't, did we?"

"Dear God, Claude and I are stuck cleaning up and dismantling, and you're off dawdling about town with your cream puffs."

"Leo, I told you, there were other patrons in need of service. There's no need to – "

"You're not paid to be *Fat*ier's personal servant, for God's sake…"

"The name is *Rat*ier, Leo. And, yes, I'm aware."

"Why the hell do you feel compelled to be his errand boy? You didn't do this for any of your previous superiors."

"*Leo, enough!* And don't ever question my responsibilities. I know very well what they entail. I'm not a slave. If I want to tell Ratier no, I can certainly tell him that."

"Why don't you?"

"Because I choose not to."

"Yes, just like with our salaries."

"If I'm ill at ease about something, I will address it when I feel the time is appropriate. You needn't wait for me. And I do no less work as a result of stopping into the patisserie, and I resent the insinuation that I do."

In truth, Edmond did once feel demeaned by being sent on such an errand, even if Maison's was just a few short blocks from the metro station. It was the first time he went to Versailles shortly after Ratier's appointment. Back then, Edmond had assumed it would only be a sole request, for what man would ask his subordinate to bring back desserts following an execution, of all things; let alone with regularity? But while this would very much be an indication of Ratier's detachment, not to mention his gluttonous tendencies, Juliette would become the justification for Edmond to oblige without a quibble. Of course, Leo knew none of this. By contrast, all that he saw was his older brother performing his duties with his usual efficiency, before strangely reducing himself to the fancies of his superior. To Leo, this was, of course, further compounded by his growing unsettlement regarding his own position.

As Claude predictably napped, and Edmond gazed sternly ahead, Leo looked out of the window: "I want to resign, Edmond," he said without hostility now, but with a fatigued sincerity.

Edmond took a moment, as he glanced at the side of Leo's face. "And do what?"

"Something else."

"Such as what?"

"I don't know."

"Well, *there's* a plan."

"There's something to be said for instinct, Edmond."

"Instinct in lieu of common sense. Oh, yes, you'll go quite far, Leo."

"I can't endure this anymore. It's not too late to make a change. To feel liberated,…like an artist."

"Artists aren't liberated, Leopold. They're destitute, and that's if they actually have talent."

"That's not necessarily true, Edmond."

"Just what sort of *art* are you referring to that would somehow make an exception to this. Wood-carving?"

"Well, why not, if I still possess the ability."

"How the hell would you expect to survive? You think carvings of giraffes will feed your family?"

"Edmond, I've given this thought…"

"You're *not* thinking. You're doing anything *but* thinking at this point. Is Michelle willing to work while you live *instinctively*? You'll be *eating* wood before you sell a damn thing."

"Well, if such is the case, then there's alternatives."

"Such as what?"

"Michelle and I've had discussions."

Edmond took a moment to digest this. "Oh, yes? And what have they amounted to?"

"As you know, her parents live just outside Nantes. They've often extended room to us. She's written to her father and the offer still stands. I can look for another line of work there, and not have to worry about people knowing…"

"Leopold, this isn't rational. You've had misgivings before, and you always come to your senses."

"These *are* my senses, Edmond. It's senseless for me to continue doing what is preventing me from sleeping at night. Don't you understand that?"

"Leopold, this is your profession –"

"Edmond, it wasn't long ago that I watched Michelle tuck my boys into bed. Every night she told them a story and wished them sweet dreams. *Sweet dreams*, Edmond. It dawned on me that *I* had those once. You know what dreams I have now?"

"Leo, I've heard this before –"

"No, you haven't heard everything, Edmond. For years I haven't been able to sleep. I toss and turn, like a horrified infant in a crib."

"Perhaps it's merely a sign that you should grow up."

"Edmond,…the other night I dreamt that Michelle's head was on the dining table. I came into the room, with blood on my hands, and there's her head on the table,…just staring at me."

"Leo, what on earth –?"

"I said *'Have you prepared dinner, my love?'* And she yelled *'How in hell can I prepare dinner when I don't have a bloody body, Leo?!!!'*"

"Sssssh! Keep your voice down," Edmond whispered, gutturally. "From time to time, it's not un-common to take work home with you…"

"That's fine if you're a lawyer or a printer, Ed-mond. Not when you do what *we* do. My God, what we do –"

"What we do is perform a service, Leo. We serve a vital function. And of all forms of capital pun-ishment existent throughout the world, –"

"I read your interview, Edmond. I'm aware."

"Is that what this is about?"

"It certainly didn't help."

Edmond took a moment, before regretfully, "I didn't ask for it."

"I know, Edmond. The point is that it's drawn attention to your name. And your name happens to also be *my* name and Michelle's name and Vincent's name and Auggie's name,…which hasn't made things any easier. I'm afraid of…what this will lead to. We could be evicted from our home."

"Leopold, that will not –"

"But that's beside the point. These feelings…aren't new. You know that. I feel that this just happens to be an appropriate time to act on them, that's all."

Edmond looked at Leopold and could not help but have a resurgence of anger towards Du Jonet for his deceit. It seemed to him that, while Leo may have been complaining more about his trade as his sons were getting older, there still seemed to Edmond to be a likelihood that Leo's words would never translate into any sort of action. But now, not only was the exposure Edmond received in *The Paris Herald* a developing impediment to his private life, it appeared to be a justification for Leo to finally move on to something else – anything, however ill-formed his plan was.

Yet Edmond could ultimately not resist taking offence at Leo's questioning their roles, for he would never have his pride challenged. His younger brother's desire to not only leave his profession, but Paris, was an expression of shame that was unfathomable to Edmond. His trade was his craft, after all. It was his contribution to his government. His country. For Leo to only regret his role over all these years was, to Edmond, a display of abject failure.

"Well, then fine," Edmond snapped. "But I will tell you that *I* am certainly not ashamed."

"I'm not saying that you are…"

"My word, do you know what the state of this country would be if there wasn't something to instill fear in potential criminals? Something to deter criminal behavior –?"

"Edmond, you make it sound as if I've just started."

"Well, it sounds as if you *have*," Edmond stressed, still trying to sway Leo's ingrained doubts.

"I'm just saying that if it isn't us, there will always be someone else."

"But it *is* us. This is what we do."

"But who's to say that this is what we have to continue doing? Papa? He's dead –"

"My father does not tell me anything!" Edmond bellowed within a hush. "I tell myself, Leopold. And do you know why? Because I *believe* in my profession. I have pride. More than *he* had."

"Well, I have none, Edmond. Not for this."

Yes, Edmond did inherit his trade from their father, but it was not as if Edmond felt his father was the epitome of efficiency. By contrast, he witnessed things as his father's assistant that even displayed a certain mechanical motivation that Edmond would ultimately grow to feel was a disservice to the trade. When one has the role of ending a life, however savage and unremorseful that life may have been, the executioner must have respect enough for the victim.

This was a standard that Edmond felt he ultimately created for himself.

"Then announce your resignation. Alright? Tell Ratier as soon as we get back. Tell him you can't sleep. That you're dreaming of heads. That you want to leave town and carve aardvarks that look like egrets. He'll be very disappointed, as *I* am, but…it *is* your life." Edmond turned to face ahead, then took a breath so that his next thought would be void of sarcasm: "I'll assume that you know what's best in that regard."

Leo looked at Edmond, and finally felt as if his older brother was at last giving credence to his feelings. Of course, Edmond's disappointment was apparent, but at least it appeared to Leo that the most challenging part was over. He would be free of this, regardless of if it led to his family's destitution. And he'd be relatively assured he wouldn't die with his last vivid memory being a recent execution, as his father did.

"Edmond,…you've always encouraged me to believe that this was all justifiable and respectable. Just like papa. Yet, I've never been able to tell most people what I do for fear of…their fear of *me*. Of my family. I haven't even been able to bring myself to tell the boys, and I know they'll find out soon enough. Like we did. My God, I've been…I've been gathering heads and bodies by your side for… I'm not immune to it. I've never been."

He turned to the window, as if gathering his next thought, before turning back to his brother: "Edmond, when…when I read your journal,…you…you can remove yourself somehow. You view this as a science of sorts. It's…I suppose it's because you have pride,…and I do admire that. I don't understand it, but I can…admire it. And, as my brother, I'll respect whatever choice you make…"

"My choice has been made, Leopold," Edmond said firmly, still looking ahead.

Leo knew this. He could only tepidly smile at his brother's commitment, before turning back to the window and watching several birds fly off the roof of an abattoir that they passed by. For the moment, he tried to see his family in those birds, and envied their liberation.

"I need some air," Edmond swiftly rose, as he tipped his hat to mask his eyes, and quickly walked towards the outside of their car, hoping that no one would notice him. Claude, in his usual depths of sleep, continued to saw the air…

***

Two weeks later, Edmond sat at his small desk and gazed out his sole window which was partially obstructed by a brick wall from the adjacent building. What little light that bled through to his residence was gray, with the sun attempting to break through the clouds on an early afternoon. It was only here that he felt completely safe and hidden from inquisitive eyes. Occasionally, a neighboring tenant in his building appeared to glance a bit longer at Edmond as he went up the stairs to his third-floor abode, but no one ever approached him. Many families lived there and, more often, seemed to view Edmond rightfully as a man with solitary preferences. But, of course, now he was never certain if there was something else there. The article had run weeks ago, but word of mouth was an entirely less predictable news source, and seemed to be trickling like a slow stream throughout many areas of France. Who knew what they knew? Who knew what they saw now? As recently as their latest assignment in Vichy, Edmond was approached by two women and a man and asked for an autograph, which he refused. It was the first time he was asked for such a thing after an execution, and it sickened him as much as the executions themselves sickened Leo.

Leopold had since given one month's notice to Ratier, and was, therefore, expected on two more assignments before he would officially be replaced. His decision had stood no better with Edmond, as their communication was now reduced to the most basic and necessary exchanges.

Hours after Edmond's return home from their lengthy trip to Vichy, he looked down at his recent journal entry, which laid upon his desk:

The 7th of May, 1913 (Vichy). The victim was Leonard von Terres, a disowned son of a Transylvanian count, who moved to Vichy several years ago and worked in various trades, ranging from butcher to fishmonger, after serving briefly in the French Army prior to his dishonorable discharge. Judging from his background, he had a variety of personality flaws and a history of demonstrative and even volatile behavior, culminating in the stabbing of a female acquaintance whom he had occasionally seen in a social capacity, after he was refused money to pay off gambling debts. And yet, this rageful act would not remain solitary for long, as he would soon after slice the throat of his landlord who merely came to his door to collect three months' rent owed.

They rarely say a word before their end, and yet Von Terres used his final seconds to curse his father, the Count, who had apparently severed all ties with his nefarious son after numerous letter demands for money: "I'll see you in hell, you cheap bastard." Yet another remorseless manifestation of evil. Once again proving that our judicial system is as perfect as one can be anywhere in the world. On rare occasion, I had witnessed regret on behalf of a convicted felon, but never was I convinced to the extent where the punishment did not fit the crime. It always fits. It is always just.

Edmond gazed at the page, before closing his journal. He stared at its cover, not unaware that his most recent entries had become more personal, in that he seemed to feel compelled to emphasize the nobility of his role. This likely was coming out as an inadvertent response to Leopold's doubts. It was simply incomprehensible to Edmond that investing years in this trade could be considered anything less than a calling.

He looked over at the makeshift enclosure on the floor beside him, wherein resided his pet turtle, Therese. Quiet, as Edmond would always appreciate, but somehow expressive enough wherein Edmond could tell if she was hungry or tired or wanted to roam about his room for a bit. Up until this point in Edmond's life, Therese had appeared to be all that gave Edmond an outlet for another mode of decorum. He was comfortable with not being formal with Therese. He needn't be dressed well or have perfect posture. He could be silly or talk to himself without fear of judgment. And yet, her presence was real to Edmond. It was not as if he considered her a shelled object that he was somehow obliged to feed ruffage to. He felt her to be a calming influence. Her slowness and utter lack of aggression was not viewed by him as deficiencies of her species, but of a wisdom that he deemed all but unobtainable.

"Are you hungry, my little friend?" he asked, as Therese seemed to have grown apathetic to the remains of a carrot that was in front of her. Edmond retrieved several lettuce leaves before placing them in front of her. He also appreciated the self-sufficient nature of a turtle. He would never have to ask a neighbor to feed her, since he was hardly ever gone more than a full day. And the fact that turtles ate at a slower pace meant that it was always easy for him to leave enough food out for her, while giving her the privilege of being outside of her box while he was gone. A part of him looked at her and appreciated what she knew and, perhaps most importantly, what she *didn't* know of the world in which he lived. In that moment, he thought of Juliette and contemplated what he would say to her the next time he saw her. Their names were known to each other now. He knew where she lived, for it was right above the patisserie. They were on the verge of something beyond diverting exchanges over the counter of Maison's, or so it seemed. He was still afraid, but, perhaps, in the next few days he would have to himself before his next assignment in Toulon, he could simply take a pleasurable sojourn for himself to Versailles.

The mere contemplation of this combined with the lengthy train ride from Vichy served to exhaust Edmond further, as he looked up from Therese and gazed at his small bed, as if sleep were a reluctant solution. He then went to his phonograph that sat beside his bed, placed the needle upon one of his favorite pieces from Claude Debussy, "Reverie", with its ethereal melody emanating from a lone piano that often helped lull him to sleep.

He unbuttoned his shirt before laying atop his bed, facing his chipped white ceiling. He did not want to close his eyes,…

It was near dusk, it seemed, and fog permeated. Edmond could not see his hands in front of his face, it was so obtrusive, but he continued walking until he could finally see the ground he was treading on. He stepped carefully, as his vision was impaired, until the ground under his feet appeared to soften. Before he could walk further, he would make out the vaguest silhouette, out of which came a strangely familiar cadence:

"Good day, monsieur."

Edmond would lose a breath. "Good day," he managed, warily.

"It's a bit cumbersome, isn't it."

"What are you referring to?"

"Well, I imagine you can't see very well, yes?"

"No. I can't."

"Do you know where you are?"

Edmond looked around, but still could not see beyond the fog. "No, I suppose I'm lost, sir."

"Yes, I suppose you are."

"Do you know?"

"I have an idea," though the voice's tone appeared to know it all too well.

"Well,…where?"

"I'm sorry?"

"Where am I? Can you tell me?" Edmond followed, with nervous impatience…

"I suppose I can, but I don't know what purpose it would serve."

"What purpose…? Look, I don't have time to waste here. Now if you'd be so kind as to –"

"You look the same."

Edmond remained, a slight chill went through him as his neck arched ever slightly forward in the direction of the silhouette. "Excuse me?"

A   wind   passed,   before   "You   haven't changed."

"Changed from what? Do I know you?"

"You don't recall me?"

"Recall you? From where?"

"*Some*where."

"I see you're quite the demon for details. But no, I'm afraid I don't recall you, monsieur."

"Well,…we have met."

"Well, I'm…I'm sure you simply have me confused with – "

"I'm quite certain," the voice sounding increasingly removed from humor.

"Then, monsieur, I'm sorry to offend you but I simply do not know who you are. Now, if you don't mind, I need to find my way out…"

"You keep a journal."

Edmond took a moment to digest this. "I beg your pardon?"

"You document your…disposings, correct?"

"My…? Who are you?"

"Well, I've told you that I know who you are, monsieur. And I know who you are *because* of what you do."

"How…how do you know who I am? From the newspaper?"

"No, monsieur."

"You've seen me at work?"

"I have, once,…but I didn't have what you'd call…the best seat in the house."

"What the hell do you mean?"

And then there was a momentary pause, as Edmond nervously leaned in further towards the ambient voice, which would then recite the following:

"The 2nd of October, 1906. (Bordeaux). Father Joseph Bruneau was executed for pushing a fellow priest down a well, in addition to stealing the proceeds of the church's collection. Money which he admittedly spent in a brothel. On a crisp autumnal morning, Father Bruneau, a term that can only be used ever loosely, was laid upon the bascule. His guilt already adding to his frail frame, quietly murmured 'God forgive my awful deeds'…before his end was met, albeit quite swiftly. I have never been so appalled. I am quite aghast at such an inhumane display from a man who

claimed to be a man of God. For if there are other so-called "men of God" the likes of this one, one can only question where this God resides…or if He even exists".

"Did…did you get that from my brother? Did Leopold tell you that…?!"

"No, monsieur."

"Then…then what the hell is this? Is this… What is this?! *Who are you?!"*

"I've been in your subconscious for some time, Edmond. I've simply risen to the surface in your dream state."

"What the hell are you doing in my dreams?"

"Do you believe in God?"

"I… That's not for you to ask."

"You did once believe in Him."

"And when I did, I still questioned His creations."

"But you didn't question *Him*?"

"I don't have to dignify my thoughts to a cretin who could not possibly be a child of God or any alleged higher being."

"I was weak."

"You were a damned fraud!" Edmond bellowed, resentful of how his faith could be challenged.

"I was," Bruneau conceded.

"You're a pathetic, deviant manifestation of everything that is reprehensible about society and if what I do helps in preventing further pigs the likes of you, then I can certainly sleep soundly."

"But you're not."

"Yes, I am!"

"You're dreaming of me, Edmond."

"Get the hell out!"

"Get out of where? I'm in your head."

"GET OUT!" Edmond screamed at the fog…

"The only way for me to leave right now is for you to wake up."

"Damnit, I'm trying!" as Edmond twirled in search of a clear passageway, as other silhouettes approached slowly from a distance…

"But I'll only return. Tomorrow evening. Perhaps in a month. It's not my doing, Edmond. The worst things I did, I've already done. What I am now is simply an image that's remained within you. I can do you no harm. My flesh is gone. My soul is in oblivion. I am merely a recollection. One that you've had many times before –"

"No, I haven't," Edmond said desperately.

"You certainly have. You simply don't wish to believe it."

Suddenly, a low, continuous moaning appeared to be rising beneath them, as if the dead were floating to the surface…

"I need to wake up. WAKE UP!!!" as Edmond harshly pressed the palms of his hands to his ears, nearly crushing his own skull…

"You will," Bruneau said, calmly. "You'll have your bread and cheese in the morning, with your coffee. You'll feed your turtle. You'll walk and hope to remain anonymous, which is no longer as easy as it used to be –"

"SHUT UP!"

"You can't control your mind all the time, Edmond. Some things will remain."

"No, it won't. I don't have to hear the ramblings of the worst kind of sinner –"

"As long as one's head is on his shoulders, these thoughts will remain."

"YOU ABHORRANT BASTARD! GET OUT OF MY HEAD!!!"

Edmond's wail sharply halted the moans and the approaching shadows, as Father Bruneau stepped out from the fog in his priest's garb, with only his torso, arms and legs intact, as his hands held his head, which concluded: "Yes, well,…at least you still *have* one."

Then the loudest of gusts came, as if the wind from the largest blade imaginable was coming towards Edmond,…before he would abruptly wake; thrust into consciousness, as only a nightmare could do. His shirt was soaked through with perspiration, as he looked around at his room, sat upright…and slowly felt his neck, barely consoled that his own head remained.

He gathered his breath, then took notice of the Debussy record on the turntable, which had since ceased its rotation. He then walked towards the window to see that dusk was approaching, as rain descended on the cobblestone streets along with the taps of galloping horses and pedestrians. He looked out at this and, for a moment, embraced that he was living – but just as soon realized that living required a return to slumber, which he feared. He now saw an existence that was broken into two halves – one was in his conscious mind, which knew well of the depravity of the world, both from criminals and now even common citizens who were approaching him. The other was the subconscious, which could visit him and simultaneously hold him captive for as long as he was too exhausted to waken.

What else was there?

He then walked to his small mirror over his sink, then stared into his own eyes, before picking up a pair of shears…

***

7

~

He had removed his pronounced mustache, in the hopes that it would do well to keep him anonymous. At least he looked less like the photograph that was published in *The Paris Herald*. But, of course, he was always wary. His trust in humanity had become all the more diminished in the ensuing weeks, and yet he managed to take the train the next day to Versailles for no other reason than to see her.

Upon his arrival at Maison's, he was distressed to see that they closed earlier on Sundays, by the hours noted on the front window. And yet, he at least knew that Juliette lived right above the store. He need only enter the side door entrance to access the stairway, which led to the sole residence on the second floor. He assumed that this was the apartment she shared with her father. Of course, then he had to hone the courage to knock – and what if her father answered? Edmond had never actually met the man, but over his visits, knew enough by his occasional bellows from the kitchen to note that he could be formidable. Even intimidating, especially to a stranger. How would he explain himself to him, should he answer? It dawned on Edmond to head back downstairs and unassumingly wait under the shop's awning for Juliette to enter or exit, but just as quickly realized that it would only put him in a position of being recognized.

He took a deep breath,…then knocked with the least amount of strength that he could control. A moment had elapsed, before taps upon a creaking floor were heard approaching, and through the door he heard "Yes?" It was her voice, at least. But now, the greater challenge was how to reply – how to explain this unexpected visit.

"I…yes, I… Hel… I… It's… I hope I have the right apartment. Please excuse me, if I'm misplaced," he managed, then just as quickly regretted his lack of coherency.

"Well,…who are you looking for?"

"I… Yes, that's a very good question. I'm… You see, I'm a customer of Maison's, and I – "

The door opened, and there she was. Her one visible liquid blue eye peering through the slight opening in the door. "Oh. I… Edmond?" she said, with subtle surprise, as she kept her voice low.

A smile possibly far too large and animated for his face appeared, as a rush of nerves came to him, "Yes, I… Juliette, yes?"

"Yes. You look different."

"Oh. Yes, well,…I would imagine so."

She smiled, softly. She then opened the door and stepped out into the hallway. "I'm sorry, I have to speak softly. My father's sleeping."

"Oh, yes. I understand."

"This is the one day we close early, so he tries to take advantage."

"As well he should, yes." Of course, Edmond still was not sure how to explain his presence, and was even more challenged by her more elegant attire, as if she had just returned or was about to depart to somewhere formal. "Yes, well, I'm…I didn't know that you closed early today. So, my apologies."

"That's fine. I just came from church. I'm sorry if you went out of your way."

"Oh,…not at all. I just happened to be in the neighborhood."

"Work related?" she assumed.

"Um…actually, ye…no, actually," he stammered, hoping that a modicum of honesty would diminish his eventual lies. "I was…this… This was more of… I was visiting someone who happens to live not very far away, and so I thought it would be nice to bring one of your magnificent delicacies to them, but I see that my timing is…not ideal. Again, my apologies."

"Yes, well,…no apologies are necessary."

She seemed to believe him, and so there seemed to be little else that she could say. Whereas Edmond had appeared to corner himself with the untrue story of being in Versailles to visit anyone other than her. He now felt pathetic in his deceit. This was all so strange to him. For someone who had spent the entirety of his adult life reserved and protective of his privacy, and whose displays of emotion were stored in a rarely opened cupboard for years, to admit an attraction was akin to a foreign language. He looked at her, and clenched his cane handle in the hopes of somehow summoning words that would at least keep her in the hall with him…

"Well, I thank you for stopping by," she managed, with a weak smile, still seeming to feel that he had a more preferred visit ahead, as she began to step back into her apartment…

"I'm sorry, I'm not…I'm not being entirely truthful."

She stopped, and looked at him curiously. "About what?"

"*You're*…my reason for coming to Versailles," he said, softly and with a slight tremble in his voice.

She, in turn, smiled at him. And, to his relief, it was clear that this was a pleasant surprise to her.

***

Edmond chose a bench in the most shaded area of Chandeau Park, just several blocks away. Unfortunately, he could ill think of where else they could go where he would not be noticed, even without, what had become, his trademark mustache. He chose a small bench, unto itself, under an overhanging tree that served the purpose of an awning for them, assisting in shielding his visibility to those who passed them on this mild Sunday afternoon. Juliette did not think much of this, even if there were other available benches that they had passed. She was more familiar with this park than Edmond, for obvious reasons. It was generally her furthest retreat from Maison's and, of course, her home. A place, as she would reveal to Edmond on their walk, that she would often come to think and occasionally write a poem, which she had heretofore revealed to no one.

For both of them, however, being out socially with someone of the opposite gender was largely waters unchartered.

They sat for the moment, the awkward silence that had emerged in the shop on occasion appeared to have reared itself again. Edmond tapped his walking stick against the pavement, as Juliette clutched her small satchel. Finally, she turned to him, smiling over her slightly reddened cheeks: "I almost didn't recognize you without your mustache."

Edmond nervously laughed, "Yes, well, that's the point."

"Why is that?"

"Well, I mean, no, that's…that's *not* the point. I was joking. Actually, it began to give me a bit of rash, so I decided to…do away with it, at least for the time being." Already Edmond felt compelled to do what was not instinctual for him, yet it was a resource he was needing to delve into more of late – the untruth.

She smiled at this, then eventually turned back out to observe the passing couples and families who occupied much of the park. However, she had no more interest in observing their lives than Edmond did. And yet, words continued to be in scarce supply between them. Edmond so wanted to resume where they had left off the last time he was in the shop, when Juliette appeared so amused and engaged by him; and the effort that took was slowly evaporating, if not for the summoning of the Paris-bound train.

"You're not speaking," Juliette said with a smile, though her observation was unexpectedly candid.

"Yes, that's... I'm sorry. Should I say something?"

"Well, that would certainly be nice," amused at how his shyness appeared to make her aggressive by comparison.

Edmond adjusted himself in his seat, as if on the verge of a significant oration. "Al...alright, um...would...? How...? I'm sorry, what exactly should I say?"

"Well,...*any*thing."

"I see. Well... Honestly, I'd prefer to hear *you.*"

"But I can hear myself speak anytime."

"It's just that nothing that I say can be as eloquent as how you phrase things. Why, the more I open my mouth, the more I'm depriving myself."

"You were quite vocal on your trips to the shop."

"Yes, well,..." Edmond wanted to admit that the shop was a bit more of a safe haven than the vastness of Chandeau Park, but it would have been an excuse that would only incur suspicion, he felt. Ultimately, his difficulty in speaking with her was, quite simply, that he was so very attracted to her. And such honestly could not be revealed, at least at this early stage.

"You said you wrote poetry, yes?" he feebly asked. Edmond would not mention that he had witnessed her writing on many occasions through Maison's front window, for such a revelation, in his mind, would portray him more as a nefarious spy than an admirer from afar.

"Yes," she smiled.

"Have you written many?"

"When I feel the urge,…yes. I often don't feel as if they're good enough to keep though."

"I hope you don't discard them."

"Some," amused at his severity.

"Well, you shouldn't."

"Why? You haven't read any, Edmond. You'd probably hate them yourself."

Edmond looked at her and, for the moment, said what felt like his first words that were bereft of artifice: "I doubt that very strongly. I don't think I could…" He stopped himself, as his face reddened, all the more apparent now that he was without his mustache.

"I'm sorry?" she inquired.

He then turned to her, "I….I was simply going to say that I…couldn't hate anything that came from you. No one in their right mind would."

"Well," she appeared to lose a breath. "I suppose *I'm* now at a loss for words," as she smiled, then turned back out.

"Oh, dear,…I suppose that means we're in a bit of trouble."

Juliette laughed at this, and in her amused hiccup, Edmond appeared to warm slightly.

"Do *you* write?" she asked.

"Do I…? I…ye…well, certainly not…not like yourself. Not poetry or anything of significant literary merit," he managed.

"But you *do* write?"

"Uh…well, yes. Yes. But just with regards to…"

"Yes?"

"They're journal entries, in all honesty. Nothing… nothing such as…"

"You keep a journal?"

"Well,…"

"How very interesting," Juliette leaned in closer, feeling that a man of esteem who could keep a journal must certainly have an exceptional sensitivity.

"Oh, not really…"

"Of course it is. It's your thoughts. I would certainly think that you're interested in your own thoughts."

"I just…I simply meant that they may not be interesting to anyone else."

"Well,…why would you think that?"

"Well, it's just… You see, it's…" he struggled to find an apt description that would not specify the content of his journal. "It's more related to my profession…than anything else, really."

"You write as part of your profession?"

"Ye…well, yes, in…in a way…"

"So, in essence, you are a professional writer then, aren't you," Juliette beamed, impressed by his modesty.

"Um , no, I… You see, I…I write *for* myself."

"Yes?"

"However, it's not necessarily…*about* myself or…*for* my profession. You see?"

"But it's…with *regards* to your profession, yes?"

"Ye…I,…yes," he tepidly agreed.

"I see. I think."

Edmond wanted to be honest with Juliette, of course, but this was simply not where he wanted to begin with her. And yet, he was not a seasoned enough conversationalist to figure out exactly how to navigate away from the course they were currently on.

Juliette then followed, with a gentle but curious smile, "Well, then…I suppose I should finally ask you,…what *is* your profession?"

In the fifth grade, Edmond was in love with Margaret Gentille. He sat across the room from her in their home room, and, since he sat two rows behind, could always see her from a diagonal angle. Her chocolate brown locks were usually what he saw more often than her face, but it was often enough to distract him. As Madame Leteré circulated random questions throughout the class, something as basic to French history as the origin of Bastille Day could leave Edmond grasping – which certainly belied an intelligence he was already exhibiting at that age. He watched Margaret from afar at lunch and at recess, having not as yet said a word to her. Then one morning, he had committed since the end of the previous school day that he would approach her and offer her some of his food his mother had packaged for him. And if she refused, would follow with an offer to walk her home from school, since he knew she lived within just a few blocks. This was the chivalrous suggestion that his mother made for him, when Edmond revealed his distant adoration for Margaret. But on the morning of his class, he started to approach Margaret's desk. Margaret had leaned into Bernard Fournette, who whispered something to her that had appeared passed on from other students, as several others spoke in hushed tones, seemingly about a related matter.

Before Edmond could step further towards her, she looked at him – and her eyes widened. It was clear that whatever Bernard had whispered to her was, indeed, about him. And as the eyes of some of the other students turned to him, it became all the more apparent that they all knew something about Edmond – and yet it was something that even *he* did not know, as yet.

Before Juliette, he thought a moment of how to phrase a reply to her question. He wanted it to be honest. He needed to be. "I…I work for the government," as he smiled with modest pride.

"Really?"

"Yes," as Edmond hoped related questions would not follow.

"In what capacity, may I ask?"

"Actually, I must say that, due to my…affiliation, I'm prohibited from revealing any further details, at this time. I'm sorry." To his surprise, this seemed the best phrasing he could manage as a means to change the subject. At the same time, he could not help but feel that this also inhibited Juliette, since she appeared genuinely intrigued.

"Oh," she replied. "I apologize if I were being – "

"Oh, please. You weren't being anything but curious, and I… Well, I'm grateful for your interest. It's just that, for the moment, I'm…sworn to secrecy, as it were," he smiled weakly, as she had little choice but to believe him. Of course, the stoppage of Juliette's curiosity would lead to another awkward silence, as Edmond resumed tapping his cane against the pavement, as Juliette again gripped the satchel upon her lap.

"I would love to…read your poetry," he then managed.

"Really?"

"Oh, yes, indeed. Do you have any with you, by chance?"

"Oh, that's… No, I didn't think to bring any of them with me, I'm afraid."

"I see," he smiled again, with subtle disappointment. He *was* indeed curious, even as they were also both still seeking ways to fill the air between them. But he felt that, no matter how wanting her poems may have been as far as polish or timber, he would find something in anything that she created to cite as praiseworthy.

"I can recite one that I've memorized, if you care to hear it," she said, as meekly as such a suggestion could be made.

"Oh, yes. Please. I'd be honored," he pivoted himself where he was more the embodiment of a captive audience.

"Oh, please, you don't need to face me. I'm not used to having anyone read…or hear my poems, and I'm not quite sure about them. If you wouldn't mind looking ahead."

He, in turn, dutifully faced out, amused but not belittling of her request. "Is this all right?"

She looked at him, then feebly asked, "And could you close your eyes, as well?"

"Close my eyes?"

She only smiled at him.

He then closed his eyes.

She, in turn, turned out as well, as if even facing him with his closed eyes was too much.

She thought a moment, then gradually, and softly, as if every line were newly discovered:

"On a day like this,
I think about what you may be thinking about.
I'm here alone, sitting, thinking.
Thinking of you.
Are you thinking of me?
Can you give me a sign?
Can you send a particular breeze
through the drapes?
This day? This week?
A sparrow to my windowsill
with a rose in its beak?
Or can you simply come visit me
for the usual reasons, whatever they may be
or for no reason...except...to see me?
I'm not usually forward.
They say it is not befitting of a woman,
but life is brief;
it is just as soon born and then withered,
like a leaf,
and I feel an urgency, while the light is here.
I don't know why I do, but it's there.
You're shy, and so am I...
but one of us must change,
at least for a moment,
before we die."

She remained facing out, as if bracing for a reaction of some kind. Edmond waited for a moment before he finally opened his eyes, and looked at Juliette to find that her eyes had also been closed throughout. His initial reaction was a sort of paralysis. He felt unequivocally that this must have been about him, and yet he would never be so bold as to voice this belief. His ensuing feeling was of an emotion he had not recalled ever feeling in his life. He was moved by so much of it; by how such clarified honesty could come from a woman of such a humble nature. And yet her creative standards were evident, thus making her all the more reluctant to share her work beyond her more insular world.

"That…that was quite… That was lovely," he whispered to her.

Slowly, her eyes opened, and she turned to him. "Really?"

He looked at her now, as if having been given just the slightest bit of courage: "Oh, yes. Your use of… Well, I'm not a literary critic, but it had wonderful imagery. It was so…so…pure, it felt."

She turned to him a bit more, "That's very sweet of you."

"Please. There's nothing sweet about the truth, unless it's a lie…or a pastry."

They looked at each other and, for the first time, the ambient life that surrounded them in the park appeared to fade. It was just them, now.

"Oh, speaking of which,…I brought you something."

Little did Edmond know that her satchel came with her mainly to transport something for him, as she pulled out a small pastry, carefully wrapped in wax paper.

"For me?"

"Of course, it's for you."

"Oh, dear, you…you shouldn't have…"

"It's without custard, I assure you."

He looked at the pastry in her hand, which she unwrapped for him. It was small, but certainly a work of culinary art. A sort of extravagant biscuit of some kind, with a touch of cinnamon atop what appeared to be a caramelized apple slice. Her poem combined with this treat overwhelmed Edmond, for the moment. The only comparative feeling to this was Christmas morning, when Edmond and Leo were boys; a memory that seemed as distant as his birth.

"Aren't you going to taste it, at least?" she followed.

"Well, it…it is lovely," he smiled at it, then at her.

She continued to hold the pastry in her hand, before Edmond managed to slowly take it from her, still strangely hesitant, as if the pastry were a forbidden elixir that might somehow alter his behavior in some way. There was also something highly unusual about eating it with Juliette's eyes upon him. There was an intimacy that now had risen to the surface, but one that seemed audacious to verbalize in any way. He noticed his hand was slightly trembling as he gently lifted the treat to his mouth, then took a most gingerly bite… The flavors were indeed unique yet familiar to him. But, ultimately, pleasurable. He chewed delicately, as he watched Juliette observing him, with a charmed smile…

"Oh…oh dear. It's…it's quite remarkable."

"It is, isn't it?"

"How do you know?"

"What do you mean?"

"Well, I thought you didn't indulge."

"Well, I have instinct for my father's baking. I know it's special,…because it's how he expresses himself." She then realized that her focus on him, while the pastry remained in his dangling hand, was likely inhibiting. "I should let you enjoy that."

"No, please. I'm enjoying *you.*"

She blushed at this, then eventually turned to a branch dangling not far from her head, as if a retreat from her embarrassment. Edmond momentarily turned to it as well, before looking back at her, then eventually he discovered an elderly man sitting alone and feeding pigeons that had begun to encircle him.

"Your father would probably say that I'm rather long in the tooth for you, wouldn't he," Edmond reluctantly stated, before looking back at Juliette.

"Oh, well,…he may. I can't say anything for certain, as there haven't been…many others," as she turned to him. "I know many are a bit afraid of him, at least from what they hear of him in the shop," she smiled amusingly. "He was once softer, but…" she trailed off, suggesting a past pain by her reluctance to expand on this. "And he's certainly protective of me, as I'm his only child. Still,…I think he'd like you very much," as she looked into his eyes, which he greeted with a weak smile; weak for reasons he could not begin to convey. "What would *yours* say?" she followed

"My parents?"

"Yes."

"Oh, well…I'm afraid they're not alive anymore, so there's not much they *can* say." Then, as he returned to the pastry still in his hand, "I must say, I've never actually tasted such a thing before."

She looked at it, pridefully. "It's an original. You won't find it anywhere else, I'm afraid. A Sweet Juliette."

Still savoring its taste, he returned his eyes to her, "That's…that's a most appropriate name for it, I'd say." His silence now appeared to distance itself from his established reluctance, replaced for the moment by his barely disguised attraction to her. "Why don't you share it with me?"

"Oh, no, please. It's for you, Edmond…"

"I would enjoy it more. That is, if it's not too familiar…of me."

"It's…it's not," she looked at him, under a whisper.

Edmond slowly extended the pastry to Juliette, while struggling to steady his hand. He was, at first, expecting to hand the item to Juliette, but, to his surprise, her arms remained at her sides while her head extended forward. He then lifted the pastry gently to her approaching lips…

"You're shaking, Edmond," she observed.

"Yes, I'm…I'm afraid I'm a bit underdressed," he managed.

"But it's nearly 80 degrees."

"Yes, well,…it's a bit draftier where I'm sitting."

She took a firm hold of his hand, then guided the treat slowly to her mouth, as Edmond observed with barely disguised fascination at her own first taste.

"It's…it's as good as it smells," she smiled, before wiping a crumb from the corner of her mouth.

"Ye…yes, I would…agree."

"Please, have another bite."

"All…all right." Edmond carefully sampled, smiled. "And the last for madame.'

"Are you certain?"

He nodded, before gently guiding his still shaking hand back to Juliette, which she again held, as she leaned in and took the final bite, smiling as she savored it…

The remaining few crumbs now left them with their hands still entwined, before they slowly parted from each other. As they both settled into the bench again, they observed the prosaic events that passed them by; husbands, wives, with children in tow. Older couples, arm-in-arm, with the occasional solitary man or woman, appearing pleasantly resigned and without envy. Edmond even took notice at how, from this vantage point, humanity appeared so remarkably unimpaired. How pure the world looked from a park bench on a warm, if overcast May afternoon.

"You're not married?" she asked, as if bracing herself for an admittance.

"No," Edmond nearly laughed.

"You've…never been?" she turned to him, curiously.

"No," he smiled at her.

"Why?"

The more he was getting to know Juliette, the more Edmond was both unsettled and intrigued by a certain fearlessness he saw in her. To him, it appeared that if there was a question that lingered in the air, she had the ability to seize it, and ultimately subvert any apprehension. It was becoming all the more clear to him that, while she may have had a similar shyness, it existed more because of a lack of societal exposure beyond the walls of Maison's. Her and her father worked tirelessly, it seemed. And Juliette appeared to have resigned herself to be there for her father; more, perhaps, than he was required of her.

"I suppose it's simply how things have…evolved…thus far," Edmond answered, with regards to his lack of marital history. He then managed to use Juliette's boldness to his own advantage. "And yourself?"

"Myself?" she asked, as if not expecting this.

And then, in a hushed tone, he followed, "How are you not…with a man?"

"I'm with one now, aren't I?" she smiled. And as her smile appeared, so did a redness to Edmond's face. What that meant to him to hear her suggest, without apology, that they were not oddities observing normal society from a distance. They were together, on this day. And with that came possibilities.

As Juliette looked out at the park visitors, she took a breath, which appeared to indicate to Edmond that something she would reveal would not come without a degree of effort: "When…when I was younger, I was…quite…rotund, if you will. To be…as large as I was was not particularly fashionable, least of all amongst other children at school who had a tendency for being..." she trailed off, but Edmond knew what she would've said, even if she did not enjoy reliving it. They were cruel to her. "Some have even come into the shop on occasion, with their wives or husbands…and *their* children, oblivious to who I am or…who I once was." She paused, grasped her satchel, as if forging on, as a forced smile came to her face. "Within the shop or my home, I've always felt somewhat protected from…what can be…harmful. And so I suppose that's why I've been…as I've been."

She turned to Edmond, moved by his rapt attention, before turning out again and looking up at the sky, as increasing clouds began to slowly form. He continued to look at the side of her face, then gradually moved his slightly trembling hand atop hers, and squeezed it ever so gently. She, in turn, squeezed back, yet still observing the sky. Before he was fully aware of it, his hand seemed to stop shaking. It was now comforted by the warmth of her.

"I'm afraid it looks as if it may rain, yes?" he managed, compelled to fill the air; not atypically to how he would do so when visiting her at the shop.

Juliette smiled, strangely, while still transfixed by the slowly darkening sky. "It's funny. I don't see it."

He now almost questioned what he was seeing, while trying not to be overtly contrary. "How is that?" he asked, genuinely.

"Because I'm somewhere else." She then turned to him, with her face appearing to have an almost dreamlike elegance to it, as if informed by an unknown source of what lay before them. "Do you…feel that way?" she asked.

And in her conviction, he understood. "Ye…yes, I…I believe that I do."

"Have you been here before? Where you are, but…somewhere else?"

"No. However, I believe…I'm there at this moment," he said, in the faintest whisper.

"Where is that?" she summoned, looking at him, as the park pedestrians began to hurriedly depart as the storm clouds continued to make their presence known. But this was not their world, now. They did not see beyond themselves. This day. This moment.

He looked into her eyes and, as if guided by them, found a sudden poetry within himself: "It's…it's a beautiful, clear day. The sky is…the sky is as blue as I've ever witnessed. There's…a gentle breeze. The leaves are applauding…and…I'm looking into eyes which are as translucent as the sea…and…I'm…I'm speechless."

They then kissed. And time, at last, appeared to stop for them.

***

8

~

Bordeaux, the following week.

Father Carnier recited, "May God Have Mercy upon your soul."

The victim, Leren Chepán, exhaled through the sack around his secured head. Soon he would barely squeal, "Ah...ah...ahmen" – which would inevitably be followed by that unmistakable gust from the plunging blade.

This time, however, amidst the scattered sounds of vomiting and gasps, applause ensued from what appeared to be the majority of nearly 200 in attendance.

Edmond looked at them for the moment, then quickly averted his face now unadorned by his mustache. It didn't seem to matter. Word was spreading throughout France, surprisingly the further from Paris that he travelled. His having been profiled elevated him, in no uncertain way, from a macabre governmental servant of old France to a mythical celebrity of modern times. Various titles for him circulated the streets, in neighborhoods which began to vary in financial status: "The Executor of High Works", "The Chopman", "Monsieur Death" and lastly, among the more notable monikers, "The Top Hatted Reaper". While he still appeared to be a fearsome attraction to many, a growing number were developing a brazenness. The more the executions continued, the more it appeared he was expected to be accessible to the public after an administration.

"Sir, would you mind?" a man of an age not much younger than Edmond's extended a piece of parchment and a pen…

Edmond would have continued walking had the man not grabbed a hold of his arm, as he was attempting to re-enter the prison. "Sir, unhand me, please."

"Monsieur, please. Just a signature."

Edmond wanted to continue on, but could not remove himself from feeling insolence towards this stranger.

"Myself as well, sir?" a younger woman followed…

"Yes, sir. Please!" another man followed…

Before Edmond knew, he was encircled, as if the so-called courage of one or two to approach him were enough to incur shamelessness in droves.

"Stop this, at once!" Edmond exclaimed. At this, the crowd stopped, wide-eyed, gasping with near amusement - as if they were at a zoo and decided to jab at a tiger, breathlessly awaiting the baring of its fangs…

On the train ride home, all remained silent between Edmond and Leopold, as it had been the last several trips. Claude, as usual, sawed the air. Leopold looked out the window, and occasionally Edmond would glance at him, knowing well that this would be the last assignment he would have with him. Now, however, he also saw Leo as the young boy he protected in childhood. The one who, among their household, would actually be the last to learn of their father's profession. Childhood memories were something Edmond all but packaged away in the deepest reserves of his memory. There was no benefit to the past, in his opinion, for nothing of it could be altered. Whereas Leo needed to remember his innocence, things that brought him joy. His woodcarving, for one, would be belittled by Edmond as a pastime, but to Leo, his talent for it was secondary to what it symbolized to him – and it was something that he was going to try to return to, despite all that his eyes had seen.

***

Edmond arrived at his apartment building, after having walked the streets at a much swifter pace than usual. He managed to have his hat pressed so far down upon his head, while shading his eyes with his gloved hand, that his obstructed vision nearly led him to getting run over by several passing carriages and cars.

"Oh, and this is for you, monsieur," his landlady handed him a letter in the foyer.

"What are you doing with this?"

"Why, it's your mail, sir."

"Yes, I'm aware that it is. And why is it with you and not in my box, madame."

"Monsieur, my apologies. I have several in my hand, as you can see. I merely was handed these by the postman. He was a bit behind on his route today."

"Behind on his…?" To Edmond, this sounded absurd, but it actually was not the first time that his landlady, a hook-backed woman of a seemingly ancient age whom he only ever knew as Madame Tussell, handed out letters, as if they were her Christmas gifts. Of course, Edmond was not of the mind to recall this in his initial reaction, for it seemed more likely that Madame Tussell was, perhaps, not unlike other residents who may've known something. Perhaps she was curious to know what kind of a person would write to an executioner. For Edmond, as with anyone who was not himself, the less Madame Tussell knew, the better. And perhaps what Leo once noted could possibly come to fruition: If she did, in fact, know of Edmond's profession and the unsettlement it may likely cause the rest of her building, she could indeed be compelled to evict him.

"I apologize, madame. I'm a bit tired, I'm afraid," he said, reluctantly.

"Oh, no worries, at all, sir. I understand. I know you travel quite a bit."

As Edmond tried to move on from this exchange, he could not depart without addressing this, somehow. "How do you know that?"

"Well,…I was only assuming. I can see the entrance, of course. I see when you leave at the very early morning and, often, not return until the late evening, at times. I'm a bit of a light sleeper, so usually counting the tenants that exit and enter help a bit."

"Help with what?" he chirped, sharply.

"Well,…with my sleeping, sir."

Edmond found his wariness putting him in a position of overt paranoia. As he gazed at the frail and ashen Madame Tussell, he knew that it was best to conclude that she knew nothing, and even felt badly that his building notoriety led him to inadvertently accuse a near century-old woman of spying. He knew, at least, that she lived a life of solitude, sequestered in the old apartment building in Saint-Fargeau for, likely, most of her existence. But his being demonstrative or blatantly suspicious of her would not help him.

It was always easy enough to be anonymous in the nearly twelve years that he resided there. He would now have this letter to blame for him being at all noticed, but it would also be the most pleasant excuse for it.

＊

He sat eagerly at his desk, looking at the unopened envelope, almost wanting to keep himself in suspense of its contents. He looked at Juliette's name as the sender, satiated by her name alone. He swiftly cut open the envelope and pulled out a small piece of paper, with a rose embedded in the corner of the page. It was the first time he saw her handwriting in something other than a receipt for Ratier's pastries. But in the form of a letter was to truly appreciate its elegance. Her cursive penmanship leaned to the right, and between the loops of certain letters and the dots atop her *i*'s, the assemblage of words was like an ink-sewn flower garden:

Dearest Edmond,

I hope that my letter finds you as happy as I have been. The memory of our afternoon together, however brief, seems to be carrying me. I look forward to your next visit. Please let me know when that will be, as your schedule permits you. Perhaps some time soon, I may be able to visit you in Paris. People may not gaze at us as often as they seem to here, though perhaps you didn't notice. Of course, I believe it stems more from envy than the difference in our ages. Regardless, ...I rather enjoy it.

I miss you terribly.

- Yours, Juliette.

Edmond did indeed notice that there were some who looked at them strangely on their way to Chandeau Park that afternoon, but was fairly certain it was not because he was 45 years of age and she 32. He was thankful that anyone's curiosity ended there, and yet he couldn't know how long he would have such good fortune. He knew enough by now that, while there were those who were becoming fanatical in his presence, there were others who were equally unsettled. Whatever their views may have been on capital punishment, it did not equate to their comfort in being in proximity of a man whose trade involved the decapitation of criminals; such was apparently the case with the visibly disturbed patron who recognized Edmond in the presence of Juliette at Maison's.

Such instances led Edmond to ponder how these individuals would feel if these prisoners were to somehow escape or be freed to resume a life of crime.

Bars alone do not solely protect citizens, after all. It was always Edmond's steadfast belief that the process of execution made the ones even pondering a life of criminality think otherwise.

He looked at the journal on his desk, and would eventually make his latest entry regarding the execution of Leren Chepán in Bordeaux, but as he looked at Juliette's letter, there was no longer an urgency to do so.

***

9

~

The following day, Edmond appeared before Ratier's desk. Ratier wouldn't arrive until the early afternoon, due to a not unusually extended weekend sojourn with his family. It was not always necessary for Edmond to meet directly with Ratier, provided there weren't complications to note, but Edmond's commitment to meet with him on this day ultimately stemmed from something other than mere reportage.

"Edmond, how did everything transpire in Bordeaux?" he said behind a plate of game hen and rustic red potatoes.

"Fine, sir."

"As expected."

"There was a bit of a jam with the blade during its initial testing, but fortunately there were no issues during the administration itself, sir. It's noted in my report."

"I see," as Ratier fleetingly glanced at the paperwork, while sucking on a hen leg.

"I had Claude and Leopold simply re-oil the slats, so there was only a temporary delay."

"So the prisoner got to wait with breathless anticipation, eh?" Ratier snickered, with a usual degree of removed relish.

"Well, of course, I had him led away so as not to prolong the sight of the instrument. We then did our standard preliminary drops. It only took a matter of minutes before I instructed that he be brought back out. Everything then proceeded as usual, sir."

"You're far too diplomatic, Edmond," Ratier replied, with near disappointment. "Sometimes I feel you should let these heathens sweat a little more. Force them to stare at the instrument of their fate."

"Well, sir, there's…really no need to prolong the inevitable,…despite the increasingly audible preferences of onlookers," he reluctantly added.

"Sometimes the citizens are onto something though, wouldn't you say?" as Ratier turned his focus more fully to Edmond, as he wiped his hands.

"Well, in this regard, I would beg to respectfully – "

"They have been coming out in droves of late, haven't they," Ratier followed, with an instant fascination, oblivious of Edmond's timid protest.

"Um…yes, sir. One can…certainly make that observation."

"I suppose you can attribute it to that old expression, eh?"

"What…expression, sir?"

"The larger the audience, the smaller the mind," Ratier guffawed, before seizing a potato…

"Well, sir, far be it for me to minimize the intelligence of the general public…"

"Oh, come now, Edmond. *Of course*, you can. Why on earth do you think we felt it was beneficial to grant a journalist permission to interview our executioner?" as Ratier knowingly smiled.

Perhaps it was ignorant of Edmond to not know that his presence in representing his department stemmed chiefly from representing terror. And, in so being, *he* would be used as a device to dissuade criminals, more so than the guillotine itself. But there was something about Ratier's phrasing that was unsettling to him; to not know a clear intent himself, and then having his very private existence become impaired as a result. It was as if a blindfolded sheep were led towards a pack of wolves, and was then asked to learn how to live among them.

Ratier continued, "The public knows what we permit them to know, Edmond. And how they react is usually in accordance with other minds. To act any other way is either criminal or insanity, or both. Fortunately, in this case, the increased audience tells us that most are reacting appropriately, supportive yet fearful. Wouldn't you say?"

"Well, I…I suppose one can make that assessment, sir."

"Well, of course, you can, Edmond. That is a very fact of our society. You must be aware that your contribution to your department, in this instance, extends to protecting our country. Why, we may be at war next year, Edmond. And what does a country do when they feel its very existence is in peril?

"Well, sir, I believe they – "

"Exactly, Edmond. They fight! But how can a country fight when some of their strongest specimens are getting their heads cut off?" as Ratier bit into the hen, as if to punctuate his rhetoric.

It did somewhat soften Edmond's feelings regarding the article. While he wasn't of the mind to take ample credit as far as the French military's options in the event of mandatory recruitment, for the moment he at least managed to feel a touch of nobility in inadvertently turning a potential criminal into a soldier, purely by the force of Ratier's words.

As Edmond absorbed this, Ratier gleefully cut into another piece of hen, "In any case, Edmond, what do you feel was the cause of the jam?

"Well, we attributed it to moisture, sir."

"Of course. We've been experiencing a great deal of precipitation of late, haven't we?"

"Yes, sir. Quite a bit."

"Well, still and all, a job well done, Edmond."

"Thank you, sir."

"And this was to be your last venture with your brother, yes?

"Yes, sir."

"Well, he's done fine work, Leonardo."

"Um, it's...*Leopold*, sir."

"Leopold, yes. Of course," Ratier corrected himself, as he continued to scan the documents before him, as if far less important than the hen he was consuming...

"He has, sir. Yes," Edmond attempted to emphasize, knowing well that, since Ratier rarely had to deal directly with Edmond's crew, Leopold was barely distinguishable to him.

"His efficiency under your tutelage will certainly be missed. However, I assume you feel confident in his replacement. Clive's brother, is it?"

"*Claude*, sir," he gently corrected. "And it's his cousin, Minister - Gerard. And, yes, he should prove most appropriate. He observed the administrations in Bordeaux, and previously in Paris. I've also placed Claude in charge of delegating general procedure but, of course, I'll be observing closely."

"I'm sure that he'll prove a fitting replacement. After all, he has worked in an abattoir, correct?" Ratier smiled at his jest.

Edmond strained his own smile all the more now, as it never pleased him to hear his profession reduced to banal quips, not to mention negate the skill that it took to not only oversee but administer a death penalty procedure. "Well, with much respect, sir, I don't equate an abattoir with –"

"And please note, Edmond, that I'm well aware of your family's vital link to France's disciplinary history," Ratier obliviously interjected. "I know that Leopold is your only brother, and closest male blood relative, and though he's made clear his adamance to sway his sons from this line of work, *your* male offspring will certainly be considered for a future post, if you and they so choose."

"Thank you, Minister. That is, assuming I...*attain* male offspring, sir."

"Girls, have you, Edmond?" as Ratier took an ample gulp of wine...

"Actually, none of either gender, sir."

Ratier placed his fork at the end of his rapidly emptying plate, then pondered: "Oh, dear, that's right. Why did I assume that you had children?"

"Perhaps for the same reason that you've assumed before."

"What reason was that?"

"I'm afraid I don't know, sir," Edmond replied, with the usual strained grin. However, he was now to a point where he wished he could be more forthright and note that Ratier's lack of recollection possibly derived from nothing more than ultimate disinterest.

"But…you *are* married, correct?"

"No, sir."

"Really?"

"Truly, sir."

"No wife *or* children."

The not unfamiliar embarrassment would return to him, "Correct, sir."

"Edmond, how long have I been your superior?"

"Well, it will be approaching 3 years, sir."

"Is that so?"

"Quite so, sir."

"Well, I must apologize for not knowing more about you, Edmond. I've always enjoyed feeling as if I can have a fair exchange of personal anecdotes with my subordinates and yet, apparently, I've been rather remiss with you, haven't I?"

"Well, sir, it's nothing to – "

"In any case, Edmond, let me start by saying that you're still young enough, so there is always time to start a family."

"Well, thank you for your optimism, sir –"

"Why, I'll even share with you a vignette which I've divulged to my constituents on occasion." Edmond was not prepared for Ratier's dissertation on the possibilities of marital bliss amidst single middle-aged men, but nevertheless indulged, as would often be a tedious extension of his duty. "My uncle was 42 years of age when he first married, Edmond. He was in the army and worked his way up to Sergeant at the time of our war with China, and was eventually discharged as a result of failing sight, which occurred as a result of a terrible explosion in Hanoi. In any event, my uncle returned home, fairly distraught, though he did obtain a considerable seat within the Justice Department. For several years he worked, keeping very much unto himself, though, not unlike yourself, taking great pride in his work. Then one day, he was introduced to a young lady by a colleague; a young lady, mind you, who purely by coincidence happened to be the sister of a man who had fought alongside my uncle in the war. This man, quite unfortunately, had returned home in a box and, as a result, the family had been devastated. But the fact that my uncle and soon-to-be aunt had this serendipitous connection prompted them to fall madly in love. They married that very same year."

Edmond, for the moment, was surprised to find himself charmed by this story, if ultimately feeling it wholly unnecessary and at odds with what he wanted to discuss. "Well, that's…that's a very charming story, sir…"

"Of course, within months my uncle became completely blind and would never again see my aunt's face."

"Oh. Well,…I would think that, perhaps, things were…still pleasant. Perhaps the mere memory of her face sustained him," Edmond grasped, tenuously. He was even surprised that he would feel obliged to impose a more joyful denouement on

Ratier's story. He even wondered where such optimism derived - then soon realized that it was, unquestionably, Juliette's influence.

"Actually, no. He became quite despondent and ended up shooting himself in the head," Ratier followed, as if having just remembered how dark a turn this story took.

"Oh," Edmond could only manage.

"But the point I'm making, Edmond, is that, regardless of his horrid demise,…at his middle age, he was still able to attain a semblance of a personal life…before it was too late. Now, if he could have first experienced that at 42 years of age,…that bodes quite well for you, doesn't it?"

Edmond resisted disclosing that he was, in fact, 45, and it indeed appeared wise to remain clandestine on the subject. He was not in Ratier's office to receive social encouragement. It was, more accurately, quite belittling for him. He indulged this man whom he respected on the basis of his title, but it was becoming more of a strain to do so. However, his loyalty would remain unwavering. He would pander to this man, where indulgence appeared necessary, in the hopes that, when he had a rare request, such as what he had now, it would be obliged without question. Only with appreciation for his years of immaculate service.

"I was wondering if I might bring up another issue, if may, sir."

"Of course, Edmond. Please," as Ratier set his plate aside, then wiped his fingers one by one...

"Actually, it's more of a gentle request, if you will. With regards to Leopold's severance."

"Well, of course, he'll be receiving it."

"Yes, of course, sir. However, I was wondering if I might request that he receive a bit more."

"More?"

"Well, sir, he does have a wife and two children."

"Well, Edmond,…I can certainly appreciate you looking out for your cousin…"

"Brother."

"Brother, yes. However, I'm afraid I cannot approve more than Leopold will be receiving. One week."

"Well, um, sir, it really would – "

"I'm afraid this is a rather difficult economic period that our once thriving country is about to embark on, Edmond. The government must preserve as much money towards military preparations as possible, with Germany behaving as they are. The President despises those damnable krauts, as you well know."

"Well, yes, I do, sir. However, I'm…I'm not asking for much more. Simply a token of additional appreciation for someone who has given most of his life to his post."

"And we have not prevented him from continuing on, Edmond. It is *he* who has chosen to leave."

"Ye…yes, granted, sir…"

"Therefore, you can see the logic here. One cannot arbitrarily be given additional compensation for ceasing to perform his duties."

"Ye…yes, sir, however, if I may, he's not ceasing to perform them for any other reason than one of his mental well-being."

"Edmond, I'm afraid that still does not justify an increase in his severance. Why, you're of the same blood, aren't you? With all due respect to your brother's affliction, this is not something that has…*affected* you, yes?"

"I…I'm not my brother, Minister. We're simply…different people. He's an individual with his own…needs and his own feelings. I'm sure that you can appreciate that, sir."

"Edmond, I can, but I'm afraid there's nothing more that I can do."

Ratier looked down at his documents, as Edmond looked at him, in disbelief that his first request for a raise in his younger brother's parting wages could not be increased in the slightest. Perhaps it was for the same reason that Ratier never really made efforts to learn his name well enough. How could he absorb the years that Leopold had committed to working as an assistant to Edmond when he, ultimately, could not say that he knew him? He was, at best, an invisible appendage of Edmond's, as was Claude. And in so being, it could not justify the minister imposing on his own department's budget.

Before Edmond knew, Ratier was finishing the remaining potatoes that occupied a plate that was, otherwise, so clean that Edmond could now see his humbled reflection in it, as he gingerly stepped forward: "And…as for myself, sir?"

"Yourself, Edmond?"

Edmond swallowed, as it pained him to have to ask what he felt should have been offered some time ago. "Well, sir, it…it has been several years since I've received any sort of additional compensation for my services. For that reason, I didn't feel it was…beyond me to inquire."

"Well, of course it isn't, Edmond. You're well within your jurisdiction."

"Oh. Well, thank you, sir," Edmond said, as graciously as he could intone.

"And, of course, I would gladly approve of a raise for *you* but… Well, again, right now,…with our current climate, Edmond, it just isn't feasible, I'm afraid. However, should things change, you can be certain that it will be my top priority. Your services to your government and country are duly noted thus far and we look forward to many more years of the same. You should be quite proud, Edmond."

With that, Ratier resumed the remainder of his meal, as Edmond watched his own dour reflection within Ratier's plate, soon obstructed by the fork gouging the final potato, as he waited to be dismissed.

So many years, Edmond thought. *And nothing?*

***

10

~

When Ratier asked why Leo did not share the same allegiance to his profession as Edmond, it was as clear as Edmond had phrased it: they were different. They were always different. In Leo, Edmond saw someone who tried mightily to not be hardened by his experiences, and those efforts were as much for his own well-being as they were for the benefit of Michelle, Vincent and Auggie. Edmond now had enough time, several days since their return from Bordeaux, to finally realize that Leopold was still young enough to live a decent amount of healthful years doing what brought him joy, even if it limited their income even more, which Edmond still deemed reckless. Of course, Edmond had no regrets as to his own life. It was only how it would be revealed to Juliette that was of some concern. For now, he simply wanted to have as much time as they could together without his profession needing to be addressed. But how long would that be? And just how would she react? There was a hope, certainly a possible one, that Juliette, who exhibited some of the more favorable aspects of his adoring mother, Lorraine, would accept it while simply asking to be told little beyond such a revelation. That always appeared to be the unspoken agreement between Edmond's parents, after all. Yes, she knew, and Edmond could tell that it unsettled her – but she ultimately loved his father and, perhaps even more, her two sons, and appeared to be grateful that they had a semblance of stability when not everyone they knew did.   It was a lesson Edmond eventually learned in his upbringing that many layers of one's life are rarely revealed – they are often suppressed or intentionally forgotten in order to live with a semblance of peace in one's mind.

While ruing from his last meeting with Ratier, the only salve for Edmond was poring over his own letter in reply to Juliette, before planning to see Leo off in the morning. He continued to read her letter, as if to assure himself of her affections, while also being inspired by its elegance, before coming back to his letter, which had already undergone several discarded drafts that were balled up like white brussels sprouts about the floor near his desk. By midnight, he managed the following:

Dearest Juliette,

The eloquence of your letter has made it all the more challenging for me to respond, since I have been preoccupied with my inability, by comparison to you, to reflect my feelings. Yet, after drafting several far inferior letters that would be better served as ruffage for my turtle, I have finally decided that I can only be honest. And in my honesty, tell you that your letter moved me so and confirmed how I too cannot wait to see you again. I will plan to be in Versailles next week, and perhaps, rather than disturb you at home and risk waking your father, you can meet me under the same Honey Locust tree we sat under in Chandeau Park. Sunday afternoon, at 2pm.

Please do not feel obliged to bring treats – yourself is all that is necessary for me.

Yours,
Edmond

***

"The boys didn't recognize you without your mustache," Leo smiled, as he and Edmond stood outside Leo's now-former residence, as Michelle led the boys in placing their packed clothing into a waiting carriage.

"Yes, I know. They resorted to tugging at my nose this time," Edmond nearly smiled himself.

"Sorry."

"Well, it's been a while since my last visit, so I suppose I was overdue for a tugging of sorts," Edmond followed, with a near regret.

They both watched Vincent and Auggie enter inside the carriage, while Michelle carefully oversaw the coachman tie up several crates upon the carriage's roof, as they now spoke in a relative whisper…

"You can't hide from the public forever, Edmond. The more who've come to know of your features, the less you'll be able to ignore them."

"I can certainly ignore them, Leo."

"Edmond,…"

"What do you propose I do, Leo? Succumb to their advances?"

"Edmond, I was just suggesting…"

"What?"

"Nothing, Edmond," Leo resigned. "I'm certain it'll all die down soon enough." Leo wanted to believe it, but it was secondary to the fact that his brother would be continuing on with his profession, seemingly undaunted.

A crate nearly fell on the disgruntled coachman, as he attempted to pull on the binding rope, "Be careful, please. We have our plates in there," Michelle pleaded, as the driver pushed the crate back.

"Jesus…" as Leo took a few steps toward the carriage.

"I got it!" the coachman exclaimed.

"Thank you, sir," Leo followed.

Edmond wanted to remain for a few minutes more, since he didn't expect to arrive as they were nearly departing, but he knew time was of the essence now: "Before I forget…" Edmond reached into his pocket and discretely inserted his hand into Leo's…

"Edmond, what the hell is this?"

"It's compensation," he whispered.

Leo looked at the considerable roll of bills that Edmond had given him, "Edmond, I can't take this from you. Absolutely not…"

"It's not from me, alright?"

"Then who's it from?"

"It's from…*Fat*ier, who else?" Edmond hushed, reluctantly.

"But he already gave me my sever –"

"It's additional. And say no more about it."

"Are you serious?"

"Yes. Just take it."

"Well, I have to write him a thank – "

"Don't."

"Why not?"

"He's…, you don't know this about him, but he's a very…modest man and doesn't take kindly to excessive appreciation."

"What?"

"It makes him appear larger than he is."

Leo smiled at Edmond's unexpected retort, then placed the money inside his own pocket, and weakly laughed: "He probably wouldn't remember who the hell I was anyway." He then looked at Edmond, who appeared stoic in not looking at him, perhaps so as not to reveal anything. Regardless, Leo seemed to discern that this was likely Edmond's money; what little he saved up, aided no doubt by a rather uneventful personal life aside from his occasional patronage to the Opera and the Theatre, along with the few sojourns that were not related to his profession. "Alright. Well, thank you for…"

"I didn't do anything, Leopold. I'm merely the messenger."

Leo fully expected Edmond's modesty. "Alright," he conceded. He was indeed surprised, and more so by the fact that his brother, very likely, after developing an emotional distance over the years, would lend any support to the new horizon that he and his family would embark on.   But the surprise just as quickly became a lament to him.

"It's a shame you didn't come around more when we lived closer, but… Well,…"

"Well what?"

"Well, I know how you are," Leo was nearly stunned that he needed to state it.

"How *am* I?"

"Come on, Edmond. I know enough to know that you've always preferred to be unto yourself."

"Leo, you know I used to visit more –"

"You made appearances because of mother. You indulged her, because she wanted her boys together. But…I know it wasn't easy for you. I know it was becoming… Well, it doesn't matter. And I'm not trying to make you feel guilty, Edmond. Things are what they are, I suppose."

It was impossible for Edmond to verbalize what it was that made seeing his brother socially so difficult. It was many things, it seemed. It was because he knew of Leo's struggles, and perhaps saw himself and Leo in his nephews. And then there was the execution of Father Bruneau, and how that affected Edmond's faith: his struggles and pious skepticism would remain clandestine, especially while his mother was alive. He *did* indulge her, as Leo noted. And with her passing in 1908, it became easier for Edmond to be removed from his brother beyond their respective trades.

Regardless, he understood Leo's perspective. This sat with him, before he felt obliged to divulge: "Yes, well,…perhaps things will change."

"What do you mean?"

"Well, I…nothing, I just…"

"What is it?"

"Leo, it's…it's nothing, really…"

"My God, it's a woman, isn't it," Leo exclaimed through a giggling hush…

"Leo,…" as Edmond looked around, warily…

"You old rascal, you're going to get married – !"

"Ssssh! I'm not…I don't know, but –"

"Edmond, that's wonderful. I'll have to tell – "

Edmond instinctively grabbed Leo by the arm, "Do not tell anyone anything. I will tell you when and if something is to become…anything, alright? But until then…"

"Is it one of your admirers?"

"No," Edmond was aghast at the mere suggestion, as his hushed tone became even more submerged. "Leo, I wouldn't indulge any of those harlots. How could you think that?"

"I'm sorry, I just thought…"

"She's…someone else."

"Who?"

It was then that Edmond realized there was no one Edmond could divulge this to aside from his younger brother. If not he, this would continue to be stored within him and, perhaps, cease to be a reality. There was something about revealing some detail that seemed essential, if not owed to Leo: "She…she works at the patisserie in Versailles."

"Oh, my… *Maison's…?!*" Leo's eyes lit up, as if having discovered the Shroud of Turin.

"Yes, sssh –"

"You old devil. All this time…"

Michelle approached them, "Leo, we should be on our way, shouldn't we? We have quite a ways."

"Yes, my dear. Just a moment, alright?"

Michelle then looked at Edmond, a sadness in her smile. "Thank you for seeing us off, Edmond."

"Of course, Michelle," he weakly smiled in return.

Michelle quickly kissed Edmond on both cheeks, then embraced him. The embrace, however, had an unusual grasp to it which surprised him; a sort of permanence. They weren't leaving the country, after all. Edmond could only attribute it to the fact that they were once just across town and now would be a considerable distance away – *but it certainly isn't unattainable*, he thought.

As Michelle went back to the carriage, Leo's regret seemed to resurface. "All of our train rides together,...and now you finally tell me something as I'm about to leave."

"Well,...perhaps I'll have more to tell you when I visit," Edmond smiled.

"Visit?" Leo asked.

"Well, yes. I thought, perhaps, for the holidays maybe..."

"I... Edmond, we're quite a ways away now."

"Yes, but you're still in the country, Leo. I have travel time in between my work. I've managed to set aside a bit of money. I can certainly..."

"Edmond,...I appreciate you saying this but perhaps that's not a very good idea."

"What do you mean?"

"Edmond,...you're my brother,...but...I think, and Michelle feels that,...due to how things've become,...it may not be wise to have you over, at the moment. I mean, I'll be working under Michelle's maiden name now, working for her father. So, in essence, we'll be starting anew. It just...well, you understand. We don't want to jeopardize..."

"Leo, that's fine. I understand..."

"Edmond,..."

"I do. That's fine, Leo."

Leo observed Edmond's disappointment, though Leo was certainly disappointed himself, perhaps more so. They were men in their forties now – brothers. If only their relationship had sustained from when they were children: Edmond always Leo's protector. His defender. Leo clung to such memories that Edmond seemed steadfast in interring.

"I mean, you were always so averse to spending time with us. And the holidays, ever since mother passed on..."

"I'm aware, Leo. As I said,...that's fine," Edmond looked Leo in the eyes now. It did hurt him, but he could not blame Leo – or Michelle. Edmond never asked for this – he only ever wanted to serve and live anonymously. And the future was uncertain for him, so why impose such uncertainty further on his extended family?

"I'll write soon," Leo gently patted Edmond on his shoulder. Even that felt strange.

"Very well," Edmond weakly smiled.

"Oh, I have something for you. Here." Leo pulled out a small wooden sculpture from his coat pocket and handed it to Edmond. "I made it for you."

"A wooden potato," Edmond observed.

"It's a hawk."

"Oh. Yes, ...so it seems," Edmond then noted, upon further analysis, that indeed there were pronounced eyes, a formidable hawk's chest and talons, as he gently rubbed his thumb along the top of the head.

"Do you remember?"

"Remember what?" Edmond asked.

"Mother used to call you her little hawk. Remember?" Leo could still not help but be surprised that this did not instantly resonate with him.

"I...I don't."

"I can't believe you don't remember that. She called you that when we were children. I suppose because she always thought you'd watch out for me and that I'd be more vulnerable to the world. As if I needed looking after, even when she was gone."

Edmond absorbed this, as he looked at the carriage. "I'd imagine that's what Michelle is here to do now."

Leo too looked at his family awaiting him, and could not help but be grateful, then his eyes seemed to travel elsewhere: "Do you ever think back, Edmond?"

"Think back to what?"

"Before we knew. When we were children?"

Edmond looked at Leo's face, and, for the first time, was shaken. He could no longer not see the boy who once was blissfully ignorant of humanity's capabilities.

"We should be going, Leo!" summoned Michelle from the carriage.

Leo looked at Edmond, embraced him quickly, as he whispered in his ear: "It's inscribed on the base." He then went to the carriage, before calling to him, "We'll write soon!"

Edmond waved, nodded, as the boys and Michelle waved back:

"Goodbye, Edmond!" / "We'll miss you, Uncle Edmond!"/ "Bye, Uncle Edmond!"

Edmond remained, as he watched the horse carriage fade down Rue Charbot on its way to their new home. Eventually, Edmond looked at the bottom of Leo's sculpture, and softly read the inscription:

"To my dear brother Edmond, Love Leopold."

***

11

~

There was something about how Edmond was feeling now. Something unusual. It was as if a door was opening to a chamber of sensitivity that had appeared to be dormant for years. It was apparent when he saw Leo off earlier that week, not knowing exactly when they would see each other again. Edmond saw what his contributions were to this, for it was very much he who kept a distance. Regret was with him, which he did not see as a strength, especially considering his trade. Juliette appeared to have played no small part in these emotions. His feelings for her were certainly transporting him, and literally so, as he looked out his window on the Versailles-bound train. The buildings, hills, chimneys and cattle that he had passed by times before had a different resonance for him now. He saw them less as part of a landscape and more with a sort of vibrancy. This, nevertheless, was odd to him. Unsettling. It had become the unknown.

He would occasionally look back in at the scattered passengers and observe their preoccupation with the views, provided they weren't sleeping. He was simply grateful that no one was paying him any attention. When days could go by when he felt his old anonymity, he would embrace it – hoping it was a sign that the mystique and intrigue of Du Jonet's article had, at last, run its course.   But he was not quite delusional to believe that, as yet. For while he may have had days where he could walk the streets without an approach from a stranger or their eyes distantly upon him, the executions continued to draw increased crowds – not only increased in size, but in volume and audacity. Perhaps, he thought, that was something that would not die down so quickly, but it, nevertheless, was something that he could ignore.

As he drew closer to Chandeau Park, he could not help but notice a woman who appeared to be following him since he exited the station. He wouldn't have paid her much mind except now, several blocks later, he saw her out of the corner of his eye, appearing to wait for his next movement, as he stood across from the entrance. He hoped that she would move on from this, but it seemed as if the duration of her pursuit had only lent a greater determination. Edmond looked at his pocket watch to see that it was quarter of two. He wasn't certain what he could do to distract himself or this mystery woman before meeting with Juliette, but he had little choice but to eventually saunter into the park. As he entered in, he sharply looked back, but no longer saw her. It was a momentary relief, as he managed to quicken his pace in the direction of where he and Juliette were to meet – the quiet bench that stood unto itself below the hovering Honey Locust tree that managed well enough to obscure their visibility. But as he navigated the paths there, he became increasingly unsettled by the pedestrians who would emerge. Most barely seemed to notice him, but he was nevertheless consumed by the possibilities.

As families, couples and elders made their way throughout the park, Edmond became lost, losing his bearings due to his increased sense of panic. Finally, as a lone woman passed him, he found himself alone – stopped himself, then took a relieved breath, feeling with some certainty that he was now in the clear. He even saw their bench, unoccupied, just a short distance from him, as if waiting for his arrival. His breath came back to him, as he gracefully made his way towards it…

"Sir?!" was called out, through an exclaimed whisper. Edmond continued on – "Monsieur?! Please!" followed, in a tone that lacked the usual sense of entitlement on the occasion when he was approached in the street. He attempted to pass the bench, in the hopes of ridding himself of an impending burden – "Monsieur, may I speak with you, please! I won't take much of your time!" the woman pleaded, now through a cracked, emotionally depleted voice that finally could not help but halt Edmond, who remained facing away from her.

As he continued looking ahead, he braced himself. What was changing in him emotionally was quickly reverting back to his anger at yet another violation. Someone, as Ratier had aptly noted, who saw Edmond as less an enigmatic government servant than an accessible personality. It would never take much for his disgust at these encounters to surface, and it was here again, rising rapidly. How he resented whoever on this green earth this was who had the unfiltered gall to follow him like a looming shadow only to accost him in the small island which he deemed sacred – the mere patch of earth which allowed he and Juliette just a few hours to gaze into each other's eyes without any encumbrances.

"I'm waiting for someone, madame. Please..." he managed, firmly. A silence came first, which was unusual.

"I'm sorry to bother you, monsieur, but I noticed you leaving the metro station. I recognized you from – "

"Yes, I get that quite often, but you are mistaken. Now, please, I am meeting someone –"

"It's the eyes, sir. I can tell."

Edmond remained, determined to not face her. "I assure you, madame, that I am not whomever you think I am. Now may I ask you to kindly – "

"I apologize for my aggression, monsieur. Perhaps...I've become delusional as the years have worn on but,...I must say that I have a strong feeling that you are exactly who I think you are. And perhaps you prefer your anonymity, and I can certainly respect that. However, if you are whom I believe you are,...I simply wanted to extend my appreciation to you."

"Please, madame, I'm simply a man with a hat and cane who is waiting –" as Edmond began to move away from her, the woman urgently moved in front of him, not to be deterred...

"Monsieur, if I'm wrong, then forgive me, but for just a moment, I beg your indulgence," she asserted without raising her voice. It was evident, regardless of her forthrightness, that she did not wish to draw any more attention than Edmond did.

Edmond finally raised his eyes to hers, with great reluctance, and in her face he could not help but see a mask of grief. He did not recognize this woman, and it was evident that Edmond had less knowledge than she in a role he possibly played in something that profoundly affected her. He saw an attractive woman who appeared to have aged prematurely. The darkness under her brown eyes signified a long absence of sleep. The whiteness of her skin sagged as though death were pulling it from her. Still, she was well-dressed. Not affluent, but certainly a woman who knew how to present herself in public, even if the presentation was just that; a façade for an absence of joy.

She looked at him for a time, as Edmond watched her eyes slowly moisten. Before he could summon the words to, again, deny that he was whom she perceived him to be, she would speak. The words would come out as if they were long stored within her, and yet they were somehow fated to be delivered in this moment, to this man, though silent to the surrounding world:

"Nearly two years ago my daughter and a friend of hers were walking home from a violin lesson, no more than a few blocks from where we're standing now. It wasn't evening yet, but it was getting dark. They were walking past an alleyway, when a man jumped out in front of them. He had a knife and forced them both into the alley. The man grabbed....grabbed my daughter and held her at knife point,...and told her friend to watch. To...to watch as he...began to have his way with my daughter. He started to rip at my daughter's clothes when her friend ran away to get help. She said that she screamed for blocks before someone would come to her aid. Finally,...by the time she found a policeman, and took him back to the alley,...my daughter had already been murdered. They found my beautiful Dominique...half-naked, with her throat cut...upside down in a waste can." She needed to gather herself, as she quickly raised a handkerchief to her mouth; her eyes attempting to contain a well of tears. Edmond remained before her, now with his head tilted down, as if conceding his ears while clearly bereft of what else he could convey.

She took a breath, then resumed, as she moved closer to him, and her whispered cadence deepened: "He'd...he'd done this before. Several girls. Eventually the police captured this...this... They captured...this man, after he'd killed three other poor girls, some in worse ways. And I was thankful when he was captured. I was...I was almost happy,...but it wasn't enough," as her sadness now appeared to merge with anger and even vengeance. "I told my husband that his capture wasn't enough because he was still breathing, and he didn't deserve such a privilege. Even Devil's Island would've been too good for him. I never thought I'd feel that about another person, sir,...but I didn't consider him one. He was...he was simply something that was beyond comprehension," she gazed off as she said this. And as she continued, it appeared that she no longer saw herself amidst the ambience of Chandeau Park but, rather, at the very site of this man's demise: "I remember the day of his execution,...how cold it was. Cold in every way. It seemed as if I'd never feel warm again. My blood was cold, my skin, the air,... Nothing was as it was before Dominique was taken from us. I had nothing, I felt, and yet...I was looking forward to this one thing: for him to be put to death. My husband didn't think that I'd be able to watch. I'd never witnessed an execution before or since but...when...when that blade came down, monsieur,...when his head...dropped off from his shoulders like a cabbage, ...I didn't look away. I ran towards him! I wanted proof that this man was dead. I wanted to see his head in that bucket," her voice clearly choked in emotion, before she let out a strained wail, as she forced the handkerchief to her mouth as if to suppress the sound... "And to this day, monsieur,...I'd swear that what was emanating from him was not even blood. It was...it was almost like tar. Black. Something...profoundly inhuman,...but it wasn't blood, because... monsters don't have blood." She wiped her eyes, her face, and even managed a semblance of a smile, as if having left the site of the execution and returned to Chandeau Park...and her mournful gratitude: "You killed the monster, monsieur. And I felt...a bit of warmth again. I felt that you did this for my daughter. *This*...was justice."

Edmond raised his head to see her eyes, still bereft of what to say or how to remotely react to such an outpouring of emotion – the likes of which he had never experienced directly in his lifetime. But his presence seemed to be enough for her. Regardless of what she likely told the authorities or even her priest or anyone who would listen, it appeared to not suffice. She needed to let the executioner know that a man he put to death was the man who killed her daughter. As her eyes continued to penetrate his, she lunged her arms around him, kissed him hard on both cheeks... "It *is* you, isn't it," she whispered, before she kissed him once on the lips...and then slowly stepped back for a final look at this man whom she seemed to resign she would never see again – "Thank you." And within seconds, she was gone, as if a leaf by way of an unfelt breeze.

It was two years ago, and he couldn't very well remember this woman. Parents of murder victims did sometimes lose themselves. She was not the only presumed mother who needed to be restrained or demanded the confirmed death of a murderer. But Edmond never had to know who they were. It was never his business to know. His role was to be oblivious. His belief was that he was merely an extension of a long-established judicial tradition. He wasn't a hero. He did not represent families or victims. He didn't need such affirmation to justify his role. He didn't need to be emotional for anyone. He could be removed, like Leo always observed. He *had* to be.

He held his face, still absorbing the enormity of what he had just witnessed, which almost served to make him forget why he was in the park to begin with,… "Edmond?" was faintly asked in the distance, before he abruptly turned to find Juliette, still, visibly unsettled by what she had observed from afar.

He managed a tepid smile at discovering her. "Jul….Juliette. It's…it's so good to see you…" he stammered, as he quickly approached her.

"Edmond,…who was that?" she remained, unusually rigid.

"Who?"

"The woman who just kissed you."

"Oh, well…I…I don't know, actually," he grasped, while looking at where the woman once stood, but had since vanished from.

"You don't know her?" Juliette now looked directly into Edmond's eyes.

"No, actually. That was…. No, I don't."

"How can that be, Edmond? She just kissed you."

"She…yes, well, it would seem so."

"Yes, it would."

"Juliette, what…what are you insinuating? That was not romantic in any way," he managed.

"How do you know her intentions unless you know *her*?"

"I…Juliette, she…she knows *of* me, yes, but we don't… I don't know her. She was… Juliette, she was simply…"

"She was what, Edmond?"

It was becoming clear to him that it would be difficult to move on from this without some sort of admittance. However, it was the degree of such that Edmond felt he could minimize, if just to satisfy Juliette's concerns. After all, she only needed to be allayed that the woman was not attracted to Edmond, nor he to her. "She was merely…expressing gratitude."

"For…for what?"

"Juliette, there's really no need for me to –"

"If you've done something nice for her, I'd like to know what it is. Wouldn't you like to put my mind at ease, Edmond?" she asked, through a strained smile.

However, Edmond did not expect that he would be obliged to explain the reasoning behind the woman's affections. This was all so new to him, after all. It was new to be approached by someone whose loss was so profound that it was a necessary catharsis to convey a gratitude, just as it was new to have a woman he had adored question him as to his loyalty.

"Edmond?" she followed.

"I…I…I rescued her cat," Edmond summoned from the deepest recesses of his imagination…

"What?"

"Yes, her…her cat was stuck in a tree nearby, and I…I managed to climb up and…and scoot it down with my cane."

"She didn't have a cat with her."

"I…yes, I…I know. The cat ran away,…shortly after."

"What?"

"However, I was assured that it knew its way home."

Edmond's discomfort in such a blatant untruth was hardly eased by Juliette's expression. He should've known by now that Juliette, regardless of her own bouts of shyness, could not be lied to. It was certainly part of his attraction to her. Not merely her subtle beauty, but her own wit and intelligence.

"You're not telling me something, Edmond."

"Juliette,…I've told you all that you need know about that…that meaningless exchange. Now I came from Paris to be with you. Is that not enough?" Edmond attempted to move on, but this was undoubtedly still with her, as he observed her gazing at where she initially observed the woman. She appeared momentarily transported to an incident she had wished she did not witness…

"Juliette…?" Edmond weakly followed.

Eventually, she turned back to him, with a compulsion that appeared to belie how well they really knew each other. It was from a place that could not be simply indicated by time, but by a deeper feeling. Their one afternoon together seemed to encompass years; their mutual loneliness combined with a sense that they were merely lonely for the duration of time that it took for them to finally admit their feelings to each other, as if souls that had circulated aimlessly for ages before being fortunate enough to meet. "Edmond,…I've…I've never felt the way I feel about you for any man in my life, but if I'm to submit fully to how I feel about you,…then I need to know things."

"Need…need to know *what* things?"

"I need to know things about *you*, Edmond."

"Juliette, why are you questioning me like this? I… A strange woman kisses me meaninglessly, and you're…you're acting as if I'm guilty of something."

"Edmond,…I know that woman. She doesn't own a cat."

Her observation could not help but reveal the untruth on his face: "Uh... Are you…? Well, then…why did you ask me who she was?"

"I wanted to know who she was in relation to *you*."

"She's *nothing* in relation to me. I told you that."

"Then why did you tell me you rescued a cat which she doesn't have?"

"I…I suppose your questioning felt rather awkward," he managed. This appearing to be his first display of honesty to her inquiries.

"Awkward."

"Yes. I'm not used to such suspicion. Just as…I'm not used to many things." He managed to feel more comfortable with such an admittance, since it at least was true, than in creating a ruse which he knew he could not sustain. Still, it was an effort to be so transparent, which Juliette could not help but see.

"Edmond, I don't mean to corner you. It's just that… It's just that, of late, I've had a growing sense that whatever time we'll have together will be short-lived, and I don't know why I've felt that. Perhaps it doesn't have anything to do with you. But, if nothing else, I feel that at least I've told you about myself. Maybe there's not as much of me to tell, but…I've told you what there is…and I've hoped that the rest of me is what lies ahead, ideally with you. But if I don't really know who you are now, then how do you pro-pose that we accomplish this, Edmond?" she asked, honestly, as only she could. Before, just as quickly: "Unless you've never had the same desire."

"How can you say that?!" Edmond exclaimed under an impassioned whisper. "Don't you know that I've never…I've never felt…" His emotions appeared to impede the words he wanted to say to denounce even the mere suggestion that he did not feel deeply about her. "Juliette, you can write a beautiful poem about your feelings, but all that I can do is tell you that what you make me feel is…is indescribable. Can you understand that?"

She smiled at this, even as he knew it did not resolve her uncertainty. "Couldn't you tell me that you knew Madame Jarnot? That you were on friendly terms? I wouldn't've been offended by that."

"But we are *not* friends, Juliette. I don't know her. I never spoke to that woman before this moment."

"Then…why did she act as if she knew you?"

Now here it was, the moment that seemed to arrive far too fast for Edmond's preferences.

"It…it *was* an expression of gratitude."

"For rescuing her non-existent cat?"

"No," he said with embarrassment. "For something else."

"Yes?"

"It's related to my profession," as he looked at her.

"Your…? Well, all I know of your profession is that you work for the government."

"Yes, well…that is true."

"I don't understand. She… Did she recognize you…?"

"On occasion, I have managed to be…recognized. Sometimes, on that basis, people feel a certain…familiarity." Edmond's every answer came with a certain hope. He wanted to be honest, but he did not want to elaborate – at least not just yet. It was too early.

"Then will you please tell me something, Edmond. How does she know of you?"

Edmond gently took her arm, and moved her closer to the still empty bench that had appeared to be waiting for them this entire time…

"How well do you know her?"

"Well, hardly at all. She's been in the shop. We've exchanged pleasantries…"

"Are you aware that she had a daughter who was raped and murdered?"

Juliette looked at Edmond, clearly stunned at the question, even as it was not something that was unknown to her. She took a moment, before she felt she could respond. Yet even the response was akin to another question: "My father had mentioned to me that she had…been killed. He made bread and pastries for the wake."

"And that's all that you know."

"I don't know if one can know anyone well enough to speak of such things in detail."

"But you know that she doesn't own a cat."

"Actually, no. I just sensed that you weren't telling me the truth."

Edmond was almost amused by this, and how resourceful Juliette could be towards her goal of obtaining information. "You should be a lawyer," he quipped. But in her face he saw no amusement. Her curiosity was even greater, and yet it appeared more daunting to her now to have answers, based on the questions that Edmond was asking:

"You do live in a charmed world," he managed, with a tone that reflected a world he had not known in his adulthood. "You've kept to yourself, with your shop, and your books and poems…and your philosophy reflects the only thing that you desire to know; a sort of…purity. The beauty within you that you…try to reflect on the world by refusing to be aware of its capabilities,…but that is not what the world is, Juliette. The world is *not* pure. It is not made up of saints, of people who simply work tirelessly, raise families. People are not simply with good intentions. If you expose yourself long enough, you'll see that nothing is without the possibility of depravity. Do you understand that? What mankind is capable of is –"

"Edmond, what on earth are you saying to me?"

Edmond was unaware that his revelation was verging on becoming a tangent of sorts, as if feeling an obligation, perhaps out of a resentment for Juliette believing in the world's sanctity. It was simply not a reality. It was a self-imposition that he did not blame her for, but was resentful of – because of what he was about to reveal:

"I'm saying, my Juliette, that...I am...the Chief Executioner."

"What... You're... You're what?"

"I work for the Justice department. I am...responsible for administering the deaths of convicted criminals."

At this, Juliette looked at him, then out, as if attempting to place Edmond in this profession; even fathoming it. She came back to him, then slowly managed the few steps towards the bench, where she sat...

Edmond looked around quickly, before approaching her, "Juliette, please speak to me. I don't...I don't know what to make of your... Please."

She looked at him again, in apparent disbelief, through a voice so soft that it only accentuated the severity: "Please tell me you're joking, Edmond."

He swallowed. "Juliette, I'm not."

She looked at him, still attempting to comprehend. "How can…how can you do this?"

"Juliette, I…I work for the Justice department."

"What you do is *justice*?"

"Yes, it is," he said, with certainty. "To families of victims, such as that woman, it is justice for an act of depravity."

"You're killing people."

"Juliette, in France, as in anywhere else in this world, people receive punishment for their crimes."

"They should be placed in jail."

"That isn't always enough."

"Not enough?!"

"Juliette, what these people have done – "

"Regardless, Edmond,…how can…how can *you* be the one to do this? *How*, Edmond?"

"Because I chose to do it. I believe in what I'm doing."

"You…you *believe* in this."

He took a moment, not wanting to speak about this without careful thought. "What I do is needed. It is respected."

"Respected?!"

"Yes, it is. Had I done something I didn't believe in, I…I couldn't live with myself. I never would've had the courage to speak to you –"

"*I* spoke to you," she painfully corrected. "After nearly 3 years, you would've never so much as asked me my name had I not first. Why is that?"

Edmond's shyness returned at this. "Because…I was afraid."

"Because…because you knew that if you pursued me, someday you'd have to tell me this?"

He came back to her eyes. He tried to have hope in his. "I was aware that there may be some difficulty in you accepting this."

"Though you hoped that, somehow,…I *would* be accepting."

"My mother was of my father. My grandmother of my grandfather. I felt it wasn't…it wasn't impossible to fathom."

"Your father and grandfather?"

"I was not merely…born into this, Juliette. I made a choice," Edmond replied, with a stubborn pride that had appeared in his interview with Du Jonet, when the question of profession by way of lineage was broached.

"A choice," she questioned without asking. She turned out, and attempted to look at the sky, while recalling, "All the times you came in, you were…you were here on…on 'business'. You…it was after you had…you had…" She was becoming sickened: "Oh, God… How could…? Edmond, how on earth could you stomach it? How could you so callously stroll into my father's patisserie after cutting off someone's head and order *tarts*?!"

"I told you those were not for me."

"Oh, yes. That's right. Custard makes you *nauseous*, correct?"

"Yes, it does – "

"Custard makes you sick to your stomach and yet you can so easily digest the sight of one's blood, which *you've* drawn?"

"Juliette, please –"

"How deeper and deeper did you want me to fall before you sprung this on me –?!"

"Juliette,…"

"What kind of person are you –?!"

"Juliette, please…"

"My God, Edmond, you're a murderer!"

"I am not a murderer! I work for the government!" he exclaimed, insulted by her accusation, which prompted him to look at their immediate surroundings.   While it appeared that some passersby may have heard the intensity of the conversation more than the words themselves, no one appeared prompted to stop. Nevertheless, it was a reminder to Edmond that, unlike their last and most pleasurable meeting, they were not an island unto themselves.

"Well, I'm afraid that isn't a very persuasive argument, Edmond," she replied, tearfully, yet aghast at his justification.

"Juliette, I…I apologize for raising my voice at you, but…please, you must not equate me with a criminal. I'm not such a thing."

"Because the government condones you to do this?"

"It is law."

"And what if they're wrong?"

"If they're *wrong*?"

"If a person isn't guilty, what does that make them? And then what does that make *you*, Edmond?"

"They have not been wrong."

"How do you know?"

"I know."

"How, Edmond –?"

"Juliette, I've been in court! I have seen these manifestations of evil. I know of their capabilities. I know their histories. *I've documented it!*"

"You've document…" It then dawned on her: "That's…that's what you write? That's what you write in your… *'journal'*?"

As her insight into Edmond increased, he could not help but feel continually laid bare. He looked away from her again, barely uttering, "I never said that I was Baudelaire."

A silence was now between them, but a silence that came not from innocent shyness. It was different and unenviable.

"How many?" she asked, with her eyes now closed and bracing.

"Juliette, please…" he softly begged.

"How many have you…executed, Edmond?"

He took a moment, then softly,…"Many."

"Many," she repeated under her breath, like a saddened echo.

He turned to her, with all the sincerity that he could summon through a whisper, "Juliette, I'm being honest with you. This is what you've asked of me."

"I didn't ask *this* of you, Edmond."

"If…if I can't be honest, then what else can I be for you?"

"Nothing. There's nothing else. This is everything, Edmond," she remained sitting, despite the firmness of her conclusion. But it was that conclusion that struck him.

"My profession is not…it's not who I am," he managed.

"What else are you, then?" as she looked at him.

"I'm…I'm…I'm in love with you –"

"Stop…!" she clenched her eyes shut, as if such a revelation were blinding.

"Juliette, –"

"STOP! DON'T SPEAK, PLEASE!" she regretted her volume, but could not restrain her emotions, as she looked at him, "Edmond, that…that man who ran out of the shop,…those people who…who stared at us, who I thought *envied* us… They were aghast. You think…you think that was *respect*, Edmond? Dear God, my father could lose his business if it was rumored that his daughter was romantically involved with… And yet you've…you've lived with this."

"It is my profession," he said, feebly now.

"Yes. So it is."

Juliette continued to look at him, before rising…

"Juliette, …I can do something else," he suddenly pleaded, under his breath, surprised at his own words.

"What?"

"I can do…I can do something else."

"You can't undo this, Edmond –"

"Juliette, –"

"*Edmond, please!*" She stood before him, tearfully. She said nothing for a considerable moment, as if the words she would eventually say would be her last to him. She gazed out, once she managed to gather herself enough, before seeming to speak as much to herself as to Edmond… "It…it was all that I could do to live when my mother died so young. It crippled us. She died by invisible hands. I was 14, and I didn't understand it. How could she be so young and whisked away by pneumonia? My father and I both thought it was a punishment by God for the longest time, for no reason,...but I realized it had to be something else. He never wanted to believe that, but I had to. I had to believe that it...it came from her need to be elsewhere. She was summoned,...and we had to be accepting of that. God takes who he needs, I felt. And I still feel that. And I know she visits us. Perhaps you think I'm fooling myself. Perhaps you think that it's a delusion that makes your work justifiable to you. These people, Edmond, they...they may be...they may very well be an evil I could never fathom, but..." She turned to him, her tears glistening in her blue eyes... "You could do so many things, Edmond. I saw so much in you. So much that you didn't even know was in yourself. And you chose... You've chosen..." She continued to look into his regretful eyes, but she knew it wasn't regret of his trade. Not really. This was who he was, in her eyes, despite however sincere he was in his feelings for her. It was that contrast in him that angered her all the more. *God* could kill, not Man – and certainly not as a profession. How dare he be the one man she would fall for. "Regardless of the 'respect' you feel that you have from whomever, Edmond, to me...what you do...and what you are...is depraved."

She took a final look at his face, before fleeing...

He rose, and wanted to run after her, but just as quickly knew the results of it. He knew enough of her to know that she could not view him as she once did. His was a world that she could never inhabit, even remotely. She could not be as Edmond's mother was – aware but intentionally oblivious. That was only a hope. He could even sacrifice abandoning his own lifelong profession, and it would do nothing to sway her now.

His face was contorting strangely, on the verge of a burst of emotion which he still seemed unable to reveal, as he watched her fade out of the park… And there he stood, excavated.

Yet before he could even process the depths of his own devastation, he sensed a presence surrounding him. Several people were now watching him, as if all the while lying in wait. It was uncertain what they heard, if anything, but they unquestionably knew who he was, as they steadily encircled him…

"What are you looking at?" as he scanned their intrigued faces, some even slightly frightened but, nevertheless, undeterred as a result of the developing assemblage of likeminded onlookers. "What the hell are you looking at?!!! STOP STARING AT ME!!!"

***

12

~

He continued to read the last letter she had written to him, as if to make up for correspondence he felt he might never receive again. Days had now become weeks and, aside from his assignments, which he managed with the usual efficiency, he was barren. Now, with her absence, he realized that while he may've not had a desire for his own traditional family, he could not ignore that even he needed someone who could fulfill a romantic aspect in him that he now knew was there, and grew to feel it without shame or reluctance. He realized he was in love with her far earlier than when he first uttered the words to her. It was undoubtedly the first visit, the first year under Ratier, that ignited something. In each of the subsequent visits that occurred, at times months apart, it had grown incrementally. The mere pleasantries accompanied by her smile and the attention her eyes increasingly seemed to give him consumed the majority of their courtship. And yet, he had only wished he didn't wait so long to act. And would he have even gone that far if she hadn't finally asked his name? He cursed himself for letting so much time pass, but his courage simply was elsewhere – if not altogether absent.

Upon thinking this, he soon felt a mild gust that emanated from the flapping wings of a pigeon that landed outside his apartment window. Even birds looked different to him now. Yes, pigeons knew death as well as he. He had witnessed enough of their demise over his years, crushed under carriage wheels, appearing forgotten by their brethren. But Edmond now saw something else, even through his skepticism. For the innocence of a bird was not dissimilar to Juliette's, and yet Juliette did also know of death – but also believed, strangely, in rebirth, of sorts. Something that Edmond could not take seriously, but indulged in her.

He remembered a moment from their afternoon, after the pending rain appeared to mysteriously dissipate, wherein a white dove landed upon the arm of their bench, nearest to Edmond. His instinct was to gently escort the bird away with his cane, long seeing it as a bringer of filth and, possibly, disease. But Juliette persuaded Edmond otherwise, merely by the touch of her hand upon his arm – as she then managed to feed it several remaining crumbs from the pastry they had shared directly from her hand to its beak, across from where Edmond nervously sat: "She's lovely, isn't she?" she rhetorically asked him, as he sat still, gazing cautiously at this odd exchange. *She?* he thought to himself.

"How do you know it's a girl?" he asked, somewhat playfully, as if trying to loosen his instinct of being repelled.

"I know," she smiled, continuing to eye the dove, knowingly, who would soon finish ingesting the crumbs from her fingertips…before departing back into the sky. He never asked her further about this, as it seemed invasive. All he needed to know then was that it made her even happier than she already was.

He would soon write another letter:

Dearest Juliette,

As I sit here, and continue to gaze at your first and only letter to me, it is difficult to not think of you or to see things that do not remind me of you. Why does it seem like we had a lifetime between us, even if it was largely an afternoon? You were most correct when you noted that it was you who had the courage, and I who needed to be prompted by that very courage to move us beyond the formalities. I have only regret about this. I regret not acting sooner. I regret not telling you I was probably in love with you from my first visit, as cliched as that may sound. I regret simply...being afraid.

Evidently, you now know the reasons for my reticence; a significant one being my trade. And I certainly cannot erase the fact that it is how I've made my living. While I don't regret this as far as my profession, I do in how it has affected your view of me.

My father did once tell my brother and I that a man is his profession. I never doubted this. I only ever took pride in this. But you

He struggled with this sentence, as an emotion began to well up in him. This was to be an admittance perhaps far too deep for paper and pen,...but eventually, he would manage:

But you, my dear, made me see this as an inaccuracy. Yes, a man could very well be his profession, but he could be something else, as well.

He could be in love, ... as I continue to be.

Yours,
Edmond

***

WOOSH! preceded the familiar thud, as blood quickly gushed from the now exposed neck of Paul Denér. The crowd of what seemed to be at least 300 euphorically wailed just outside Le Gant Prison in Bordeaux, as if this death were their own personal victory. Claude and Gerard gathered Denér's remains, as Edmond looked out at this latest gathering of townspeople, now too numb to feel any rightful contempt, but cognizant enough to see that most had no tangible connection to Denér or his murderous crimes. What they *did* seem to have was an immeasurable desire to be entertained. What was even more stunning was that this appeared to be the one event that tethered the wealthy and the poor. Somehow, in these eyes that Edmond continually looked into from afar, the execution was the one event that lacked a class delineation. For the poor, it always seemed clear enough that an execution could, perhaps, make the lugubriousness of their own lives seem to pale by comparison – as if to say, *Well, at least I still have my head!* But the growing masses of the more affluent told another story, but one that, in the end, Edmond could not be surprised by. He now could clearly see, as he noted with Ratier, regardless of the financial and familial accoutrements that could adorn one, that it was never enough to truly fulfill: These being the same people who dutifully attended Sunday mass, who gave the sign of the cross when passing a church, who undoubtedly went to great lengths for celebrations of baptisms, confirmations and weddings, all under the name of God.

There is no God, Edmond thought, his belief all the more affirmed of this as he watched them. *How could there be?* He continued to watch their eyes and cheers that had become silent to his ears, as he stood beside his guillotine. Father Bruneau, the priest who occasionally visited Edmond in his dreams, played a part in Edmond's skepticism, but Edmond would still insist that it was never his trade that thwarted his beliefs. For if God existed, He would believe in punishment and the culpability of the sinner. *But what could God or a god make of crowds salivating for the demise of another, even a remorseless criminal?* It was human behavior and the proof, in such behavior, of a true absence of soul, despite one's so-called religious allegiance. He was convinced that much of the world, or at least of France, was occupied by hypocrites. Any sort of piety was merely a shield that would protect them from the guillotine, without their making any efforts, aside from the counting of rosaries, towards a truly fulfilling existence.

And yet, here they all were; in Bordeaux, in Paris, in Versailles, in Vichy…

Men, women, young, old, rich, poor… Here they all were.

***

"Versailles, on the 22nd of June, Edmond," Ratier spouted, as he handed him the pertinent documents.

Edmond stood there, momentarily stunned by the mere mention of Versailles. This would be his first return back since his last meeting with Juliette in Chandeau Park the previous month. And since, he had written her countless letters, all to no avail. He didn't dare return to the shop on his own, as a result of sensing her unequivocal adamance. After all, it was all that he could do to make the efforts he did during their courtship, culminating in his pledge of love for her. But it was all the more foreign to him to persist despite her rejection. He felt letters were at least less of an imposition for her, but to arrive in person would be something else altogether. And now he didn't seem to have a choice.

"Twelve of those delicious eclairs, Edmond, along with three palmiers and three lemon custard tarts," Ratier requested, with unbridled delight. Edmond looked at Ratier's ridiculously grand smile, and, in the moment, could not fathom how he could avoid this excursion. It had been the one errand he would undertake for Ratier, which he had been doing without resistance since Ratier's appointment, so it would only be odd for him to suddenly refuse. He had been the very definition of allegiance, and so what reason could he now give to not indulge his superior's emphatic vice? He could only dutifully jot down Ratier's request, as always, while internalizing a contempt that he started to have for this man that he would likely never reveal. He could only hope that this affluent behemoth before him would quickly be seized by a heart attack and just as soon be replaced by a new minister who cared only for the results of Edmond's work and less about dessert. One who might even grant him his long overdue wage increase.

As Ratier, through nibbles of a well-basted chicken leg, rambled on about a recent trip he and his family had taken to their villa in the country, Edmond could only think of how he would walk into Maison's now. What he could say. Perhaps he could send Claude or Gerard in his stead, but that simply defied his own ethics regarding the functionality of his crew. He had compromised enough, he felt, and had done so without so much as a pay raise. And yet, if not for Ratier's requests, Edmond would have never encountered Juliette. He would've never had the chance to even spend one precious afternoon together, alone, under a shaded tree with her. But what did that all mean when it would appear to end just as suddenly? *Perhaps...just perhaps, it is fate that forces me to return to her,* he thought.

Perhaps there is hope, still.

***

WOOSH! – preceded the familiar thud, as blood quickly gushed from the now-exposed neck of Marcel Mauret, to a thunderous roar. It was becoming increasingly difficult for even Claude to ignore the audience sounds, which was significant considering how undaunted he usually was. That, combined with Gerard's lack of experience since taking the place of Leopold, made Edmond that much more frustrated by how the public euphoria was taking precedence over the intended function of the executions.

"Rot in hell, bastard!"

"Thank you, Monsieur Decapitator!"

"Maybe the devil will have your head for you!"

"Bravo, Chopman!"

The audiences now lingered in greater amounts. Their words of both praise for Edmond and condemnation of the prisoner lingered amidst inaudible exultations that appeared perpetual. As Claude and Gerard gathered Mauret's remains, Edmond could no longer observe without the audience idling towards him like a tide that creeped up the shoreline:

"Monsieur, may I – ?"

"Sir, would you mind signing – ?"

"Monsieur de Capitoir, would you – ?"

Before Edmond swiftly barked, "Get the hell away! This isn't a damn performance, you imbeciles!"

They would only be slightly dissuaded, yet most seemed more intrigued, despite any fear they may have exhibited. It was even beginning to incur in Edmond a near violent tendency, as he was now reduced to swinging his cane just to keep a distance from the townspeople. This appeared to be the next stage of demonstrative necessities that may have very well soon needed to be followed by a flaming torch.

"A man has died!" he would follow, as he swung his cane.

"A devil is what he was!" yelled one.

"And do you even know what he did, you fools?! His name?!" Edmond angrily followed.

"He's been executed, for Godsakes. That's enough!" yelled a woman, who appeared to be as passionate as she was ignorant.

Many didn't know, in fact. Yes, some read the papers which would usually announce the execution, and thus the scant details would usually be provided within, but Edmond soon came to discover that many didn't know anything of the victim, other than that they were condemned. The more they appeared to come, the more it was likely that the many who observed were simply becoming swept up in a sort of pandemonium.

Suddenly, the pace in which Claude and Gerard needed to clean up and dismantle had to increase, just as Edmond needed to be more creative in departing.

***

Edmond managed to covertly take a carriage to Rue Chablés, and strategically departed a half a block from the entrance to Maison's. With his hands covering much of his face, he quickly made his way across the street and placed himself in the usual corner of the window, where he could peek inside without being seen. He very much felt Versailles's eyes upon him. And yet the only one whose attention he truly sought seemed to want nothing to do with him. *But how could this trip exist without purpose, other than as another assignment?* he wondered. On the train to Versailles, she was all he could think about. At one point, by the time of their arrival, he was even hopeful that, in seeing him, and some weeks passing, her resistance would be lowered and she would manage to, at least, hear him – even if he no longer knew what words he would say.

He watched her tend to two frail women, who soon gathered their box of pastries with some effort. Then, to his surprise, Juliette came from behind the counter to open the door for them, since their hands were full, as Edmond stood up and hid himself against a neighboring façade upon hearing the door's familiar bell. He watched the elderly women fade down the street, before crouching and peeking inside again. Juliette would return behind the counter, sit on her stool and then would write something in her journal, which he had fleetingly noticed in the past. *Could it be a letter to me?* he hoped. *A poem, even?*

He wanted to watch her forever, but time and his surroundings were adverse elements. Pedestrians would pass, and he would hide his eyes with his hat. A carriage, car or cyclist would pass, and he would make sure his back was exposed. All the while, he watched her, and gripped his cane in search of an answer. *What should I do?*

He then recalled the last few lines from the poem she had recited to him:

> *You're shy, and so am I...*
> *but one of us must change,*
> *at least for a moment,*

before we die.

It made his decision for him. He motioned for the door, before fear could take hold…and then, just as his eyes met Juliette's:

"There he is!" yelled a pedestrian from across the street…
"Oh my God!" followed another…
"The Reaper eats pastries, apparently," another whispered aloud…
"Oh, my Lord – it's Monsieur Death!" wailed another, with horror…

Edmond stopped, turned to see a gathering of people across the street, all observing his entrance as if he were on exhibit, as their exclamations died down to a trembling sea of murmuring. Several others stopped to look at him, which soon became much of Rue Chablés; even local tenants leaned out of their apartment windows above. He became paralyzed by their gaze, as he remained with his hand on the opened door, before turning back inside the shop to see Juliette observing all of this– as was evident in her appalled eyes and agape mouth. A sudden deafness came to Edmond. He could only see, but what he saw was Juliette's horrified expression, as she seemed to move further away from him. But, in actuality, it was Edmond seeing her as if he were floating backwards, to the point where she was becoming increasingly distant. And, eventually, amidst the shattering silence, he would not see her at all. It was emblematic of the chasm that was now between them.

It's over, he thought. And in this admittance, it was as if what remained of his heart was all but excised from him.

At that point, Edmond saw nothing left to do but flee to Gare de Versailles…

***

13

~

Weeks had elapsed, with Edmond living and working in a state of rote catatonia. It was reported that, due to the growing visibility of the executions, crime throughout much of the country was seeing a dramatic descent. This, according to Ratier, was the plan all along: to deter crime and, thus, maximize the manpower that France would have in the event of a war with Germany, which seemed increasingly likely. But Edmond could take no solace in this now. If he felt much of the country, not to mention his superior, were soulless, then he had surely come to see himself as a device driven by such moral absence. While his doubts as to the existence of God had resided within him for some years, he did always believe in morality, and could always take pride in his profession and the role that it played – it was what his father always preached, after all: *A man is his profession*, and everything else was secondary. Perhaps it was his father's own justification for not being the most present parent, or the most present husband, for that matter,...but Edmond believed it. He believed it enough for it to sustain him for these many years – but then came Juliette into his life, albeit in moments. But ultimately it was enough to make an impact on him. It was enough for him to even believe that he could marry his trade with the ability to love a woman.

Leopold managed it, and Michelle endured well enough, but it was always a great struggle – even more for Leo.   Edmond could see that all the more now. And yet, as Juliette once posed: What was he, truly? He was his profession – and now, in his mind, it had come in conflict with other desires – desires that could make him feel a sense of fulfillment he had disregarded but, nevertheless, enjoyed.   Yet it was not enough for him to simply know that he could love someone – he had loved Juliette, and he was certain of that. But she did not love him anymore,…and he was fairly certain of that, as well.   Now he resented having been exposed to such feelings.   He resented her.

He would complete his most recent journal entry, which were becoming less about a victim's background and more about his contempt for the onlookers, in addition to the recent articles in *The Paris Herald* and other newspapers that were noting of Edmond nearing his 500th execution, as if he were an athlete on the verge of some sort of unprecedented milestone:

This is a country void of a center, and yet we seem to be secretly preparing for a war against a neighboring country that lacks the same. But I can only speak for France now, for I am within it and am seeing it. I am seeing that the sentenced are becoming less human to me. They are mannequins with criminal records. I don't even care to know about them or their crimes anymore. I don't need to hear their sentencing to justify their deaths. The justice department has never cared to hear any reportage from me. And the savage onlookers only care to be entertained. I know there are mothers like the one I met that day in Chandeau Park who see this differently, but they are a considerable and indiscernible minority. France consumes them like Ratier consumes game hens.

And now Philippe Du Jonet and others have audaciously taken a salary to report that I will be executing my 500th soon. It will be a spectacle, undoubtedly.

There seems to be little choice for me then to be the lamb ingested by all of this. Not even a government servant. Not even a man. And no longer loved.

He placed his pen down and looked at this entry, then looked at the window which revealed nothing but the brick wall from the neighboring building that partially obstructed the overcast light from coming through,…before looking back at the page.

He then thought, if he was indeed his profession and nothing else, there had to be a solution other than simply abandoning it. *And for what, exactly?* He knew nothing else. This is what he knew. This is who he was. This is likely who he would always be.

And then it came to him.

***

As the largest crowd to date gathered outside Strasbourg Prison, Edmond strangely came out from the prison entrance ahead of Claude, Gerard and the prisoner, Rafael Alouít. Claude and Gerard were fairly clueless as to what Edmond had in mind, as they were only told: "Wait until I give the signal."

"The signal?" Claude asked.

Edmond said nothing else.

It was highly unusual for Edmond to come out alone, especially since he had long been unwavering regarding his established protocol. The clamoring crowd was soon hushed by his sole presence, alongside the guillotine that was recently erected. They knew, for certain, it was him – as he had allowed his mustache to grow back in recent weeks, though it still hadn't approached its usual size. Edmond seemed content to disguise nothing. He held a crate in one hand and his walking stick in the other. He lacked his own ingrained persona which, until now, had been unequivocally reserved. By contrast, his chest was more pronounced, as if he were imposing on his own body a fearlessness that was never before exhibited. He no longer seemed introverted or clandestine or even quietly mythical. He projected something altogether different.

He placed the crate upon the ground, looked at the surrounding audience with widened eyes, piercing with both a menace and a strange showmanship. The silence was deafening, conveying the crowd's utter confoundment as to what was to come. He then leapt upon the crate, raised his cane to the sky, as if about to summon thunder, then bellowed:

"Step right up, monsieurs and madams!
And watch the heads fall like cabbages
into this can!
For I can turn a sinner's life so quickly

into death
for crimes ranging from murder, rape
and theft!
No one in Europe is quicker with the blade!
A standard which no one before me has made!
Now listen and watch with depraved
fascination
at the art and skill with which I perform this
decapitation!"

The silence remained, for it was simply too stunning for the audience to grasp. Now the "entertainment" was actually acting as such, as opposed to a capital procedure that had become a morbid intoxicant. The executioner was now an unbridled master of ceremonies. He gazed out at them, knowing well that he could not flee from his outburst. He could only wait for a result of some kind. It dawned on him, in this frozen moment on a humid August day, that they may well have preferred the Edmond de Capitoir of old: rigid, enigmatic, unwelcoming. This exhibition could very well prove his undoing – and yet, he felt he had little to lose. He at least felt his years of service were owed him asserting some control over circumstances that he had become victimized by. He didn't have his own family, after all. He didn't have a woman who loved him anymore. He needn't cling to his father's old school philosophies of what made a man. He had nothing but a turtle and some integrity that he could hold onto, even if it led to his immediate dismissal.

He continued to gaze at them, audaciously, as the seconds seemed to grow into minutes,...before it came: A deep and thunderous ovation from the crowd who was not only surrounding outside of the prison, but even seeping into several adjacent streets. The ovation and tremorous roars built and became unrestrained. Hands were thrust in the air. The photographers beside Du Jonet and the other neighboring journalists began taking photographs, as the flashbulbs exploded into the air like a sudden assault of grenades.

Edmond raised his cane and then dipped it like a conductor silencing his orchestra, as Claude and Gerard gazed on from inside the prison entrance:

"What the hell is he doing?" Gerard exclaimed.

"He's gone mad," answered Claude, appearing as stunned as he could be under his cavernous face, as his hand remained around the prisoner's arm, who seemed too preoccupied with his own fate to give much thought to the unbecoming events outside.

"Are you ready?!" Edmond wailed to the masses.

"YES!!!" the crowd answered.

"Are you ready?!" Edmond followed.

"YES!!!" the crowd answered.

"Are you ready?!!!"

"YEEEEEEEES!!!!!!!"

The flashbulbs from the newspaper cameras were re-ignited, as the calls for the latest head were now beyond decibels…

Edmond signaled for Claude and Gerard to bring out the prisoner, Rafael Alouít; a career thief and forger; though exactly how much was known of Alouít and the crimes he committed among the town was speculative.   In truth, it didn't matter. He was sentenced and that was good enough, as Edmond now knew well. But Edmond's ringmaster persona had taken him over – a creation that made the proceedings, and the tumult that surrounded it, tolerable. And it was only that because he was no longer himself. His sense of respect for the procedure and his efforts for the sentenced to undergo it as swiftly and painlessly as possible were now submerged beneath what he had now become.

WOOSH! – was followed by the ever-reliable thud, signaling the successful descent of Alouít's head into the sawdust-filled bucket. No sooner had Claude and Gerard gathered his remains, than did Du Jonet and several other lesser-known journalists, along with their photographers, encroach along with a considerable portion of the townspeople. Now the prison guards and several nearby constables were needed to prevent the approaching crowd from stampeding, who were all the more intoxicated by Edmond's showmanship, and aggressive in their pursuit of autographs…

As Edmond willingly dispersed his signature and accompanying salutations to the faceless, while remaining atop the self-invented stage, he fielded questions from Du Jonet and the other surrounding press, as the camera flashbulbs continued to ignite:

"It appears as though you've developed an immunity to the camera, Monsieur de Capitoir," Du Jonet inquired, with a sustained if stunned grin.

"I suppose one can acclimate to anything, if they so desire," as Edmond signed with an unbroken yet heightened glee…

"Yes, so it would seem," Du Jonet noted.

"You executed your 500th this morning, is that correct?" another journalist followed.

"Well, you're the reporters, yes? I assume you'd know more, as I admittedly haven't had the time of late to make my own count."

The reporters laughed, surprised and yet relishing how amenable Edmond was to their inquiries.

"Do you have any opinion on today's victim, sir?"

"An opinion? Well, let's just say that I wouldn't have him over to meet my mother."

More laughter followed, as Edmond continued to churn out autographs at a pace almost as swift as his guillotine skills…

"Do you attribute the decline in criminal behavior to your recent ascent in popularity?" Du Jonet followed.

Edmond could not help but to look at Du Jonet directly on this particular question: "Well, Monsieur Du Jonet, I suppose that if you wish to credit me than you also wish to credit *yourself*, yes?"

Laughter continued, though Edmond could not help but take a certain satisfaction of it being at Du Jonet's expense.

"Do you foresee an abatement in the number of executions in the near future, as a result the decreasing crime rate?" asked another reporter.

"Possibly so. But one thing that I believe will not change, gentlemen, is the presence of the inherently nefarious. And while there remains such, despite a seemingly dwindling number, I imagine there is little for France to do but to educate by means of capital punishment," Edmond replied. Then just as quickly handed another autograph to a young woman, "Thank you, madame."

"Thank you, sir!"

Du Jonet would interject: "You seem to have, of late, embraced your newfound celebrity, monsieur. This is a considerable departure from the reticence I recall from our initial interview."

"I don't know if 'embraced' is the most accurate terminology. More is it a modest acceptance," as he handed off another autograph: "There you are."

"May I ask what has prompted such a change?" Du Jonet followed.

"You may ask but I'm not required to tell you," Edmond replied with a smile, as he returned another pen and autograph to the faceless mass…

"Could it be a sort of epiphany?" asked another journalist, garnering ambient laughter, as a result of the French holiday of the same name, which celebrated the visit of the three Wise Men to the infant Jesus.

Edmond heard this and, for the moment, thought of Juliette. He remembered a story she had told on their wonderful afternoon in May, when her father would make her and her mother a sumptuous cake. Traditionally, it was designed to have coins inside and the discoverers of such would then be pronounced kings for the day. This was indeed something that Edmond recalled from his youth, when he and Leopold would be pronounced such by their mother. But since Maison's family was made up of his wife and sole daughter, he would disregard the male tradition. Instead, he would hide two coins for them to find, and, upon their discovery within the cake's layers, would pronounce them *queens* for the day, yet noting it as merely a formality – for, as Juliette recalled, he had always considered them such.

Edmond needed to quickly remove this from his memory, as he came back to the journalist's question, with a widened if feigned smile: "An epiphany?! Sir, let's just say that one only lives once, despite myths to the contrary," as he completed another autograph. His reply would be quizzical to the reporters, and far too vague to probe in such a setting – but it needn't have mattered. Edmond was simply denouncing a belief in anything. He was denouncing everything that he felt could soften him amidst his surroundings.

"Sir, it looks as if Roland Marque is set to be put to death at your swift and able hands. What are your thoughts on this?"

Edmond knew the scant details of what had been disclosed by Ratier; those being that Roland Marque was recently sentenced to die for the rape and murder of several teenaged girls, all within the last few months. But what gave this case particular distinction, and what no doubt expedited his date of execution, was that one of the girls happened to be the daughter of Paris' governor. It was undoubtedly going to be the most profiled execution of Edmond's career, but one that did not register with him as anything more than a future assignment.

"I have no thoughts on this, sir, other than that, with his sentence being confirmed, he will be assured a swift and just punishment," as he handed off another autograph to a seemingly affluent couple, who would then feel compelled to euphorically recite it aloud:

"Keep your head on your shoulders – Monsieur de Capitoir!!!"

***

14

~

Du Jonet's article would be printed in *The Paris Her-ald* that week. His coverage initially was deemed notable for it being Edmond's 500th so-called 'victim', but would become all the more so as a result of Edmond's galvanizing display prior to and after the execution of Rafael Alouít. As a result, his usual flair for dramatic license in his reportage would be hardly necessary:

Call him "The Chopman", if you will. Call him "The Executor of High Works". Call him "The Top Hatted Reaper". Regardless of one's preferred moniker, France's mythically renowned Edmond de Capitoir was in the rarest of forms right before this journalist's awestruck eyes in Strasbourg. With a ringmaster's vibrance, de Capitoir not only leapt atop his makeshift stage, as if the opening act for the ma-cabre main event of execution, but would orate in rhyme, as if the explosion of a well-submerged Bau-delaire that had heretofore been in hiding. Yet none of this altered his efficiency in the slightest – and no sooner did he successfully decapitate Rafael Alouít, a career thief and forger – than did de Capitoir not only answer inquiries with near merriment, but elect to sign autographs for the massive crowd that had, up until now, seemed to have become expectant of his more clandestine mystique.

This journalist can only wonder what prompted such a herculean shift in persona from our initial meeting earlier this year. And he can only be equally intrigued by what is to come.

Edmond read the article at his desk in his apartment. As if the words weren't enough, they were alongside a photograph of him atop his crate waving his cane into the air. It was someone else, he observed. Not him. It was the only logical belief.

He turned to Therese, who was near his feet, and envied her ignorance despite her ability to live for decades; then turned to his window, as if waiting for something to arrive, but again was only greeted by the thin stream of obstructed light bleeding in. He wasn't sure what he was expecting, anymore. Perhaps anything but the nothing that was there.

He then came back to the article, pushed it out of his vision. He then urgently grabbed a sheet of paper and a pen:

Dear Leo,

He stared at this for a long time, and could not think of a word to follow. What could he say to his brother now, who already did not want to be reminded of his old profession, much less be tethered to his brother's reputation. And now there was this article, if he ever came upon it, not to mention the other smaller newspapers that were in attendance. Admittedly, Edmond hadn't thought of Leo prior to his exhibit at Alouit's execution. It would only be a greater shame to him. Edmond at least knew that Juliette might never know of this, since her and her father were relatively closed off to the outside world beyond their shop – but he knew the outside world came in. Who knew what they knew, or what they could even say? Edmond knew his was a selfish act, but he saw little recourse other than to bathe in his loneliness and sense of abandonment. Not just by Juliette, but by Leo, his only brother.

Ratier, to Edmond's surprise, was undeterred by Edmond's display, rationalizing that the more that would attend these executions would only aid in the diminishment of crime. To Ratier, it was simply about numbers and notarization. And Edmond's efficiency would always reflect well on his department. It was as simple as that. Now his seeming goal was to assure that the Justice Department would execute those deserving, and continue to instill fear, even through the guise of what was becoming a vaudevillian display. He didn't seem to care what Edmond did, or what happened to the prisoner, so long as they didn't somehow escape to add to the crime statistics.

And so, once again, all that Edmond appeared to have was his profession,…whether he wanted it or not.

***

"AAAAAAAAAAAH! MY GOD! OH MY GOD, PLEASE HELP ME! PLEASE PLEASE END THIS! PLEASE! AAAAAAAAAAAAAAAAAAAAAAAAAH! AAAAAAAAAAAAAAAAAHHHHH!!!!" bellowed

Roland Marque, much to the silenced shock of the on-lookers outside Le Sante Prison. Claude and Gerard could only look at Edmond, helplessly, as Edmond looked aghast at what he was seeing: somehow, the slats by which the blade descended were insufficiently lubricated, leading to a halt in the momentum of the blade and, thus, it managed to only make it halfway through Marques's neck. His desperate screams sounded like they could be heard throughout Paris, even through the sack upon his head, as Edmond turned briefly to the crowd, saw them still and rapt, before urgently turning back to his crew...

"Raise the blade, Claude," Edmond ordered.

"Raise it? How –?"

"With the damned rope, man! Raise it up!"

Since the blade was already down by way of the lever, it needed to be pulled up by the rope, as was normal procedure. However, it was not normal for the blade to still be within the neck of the prisoner, and that very abnormality reduced Claude and Gerard to a stunned immobility.

"Damnit, get out of the way!" Edmond rushed to the rope, as Marques continued his unbroken stream of desperate pleas... Edmond yanked the rope, as Claude and Gerard watched on, but the blade would not budge. It seemed to only incur more pain the more Edmond desperately yanked. "DAMNIT!" he screamed, as audible murmurs of shock permeated the captivated audience, while Marques continued pleading to God...

Finally, Edmond urgently looked at the slats, and how the blade was rendered immobile by its current position, and saw no other choice but to jump atop the blade and, by sheer manual force, finally managed to completely remove Marques's head - which descended into the bucket, his silence now matching that of the hundreds in attendance.

As Claude and Gerard resumed their normal practice of gathering the body in its basket, Edmond watched, but for the first time, was truly beside himself. It was someone else who must've performed this act of savagery, not him. He then looked out at the crowd, who, at first, he assumed would depart in nauseated silence,…but to his surprise, it appeared as if it took just a moment for them to digest what they had witnessed, before erupting in applause and primal caterwauls, the likes of which Edmond had never heard…

"GET THEM AWAY, AT ONCE!" he yelled to the nearby constables, who were now increased in number due to the expected turnout.

As many townspeople attempted to approach him, "GET AWAY FROM HERE! GO BACK TO YOUR HOMES, DAMNIT!" as Edmond waved his cane wildly to keep them away, while the policemen tried desperately to herd the oceanic crowd. At the same time as all the hysteria, Claude and Gerard worked as quickly as possible to remove Roland Marque's remains from sight. "Rot in hell, you bloody cretin!" yelled a man, who even picked up the bucket as Claude and Gerard were removing his body, which forced Gerard to drop Marques's legs and urgently rush towards the man, who now pulled the head sack out and held it up – "Look at the body you can no longer use, you beast!" as primal cheers followed.

Gerard grabbed the sack from him angrily, "Get out of here, you bastard!"

After several minutes, much of the crowd had dispersed, leaving an exhausted but enraged Edmond to finally chastise his usually efficient crew:

"What on this earth was that?! WHAT ON THIS GREEN EARTH JUST HAPPENED?!!!"

"The blade jammed," Claude answered, still clearly shaken.

"Yes, I am aware that it jammed, Claude. *Why* the hell did it jam?!"

"I suppose the slats weren't –"

"I know the technical rationale for why it jammed, Gerard! You both were in charge of making certain that all was in working order before the administration. Why wasn't that done?"

"Edmond, we –"

"I don't want excuses, Claude. *Why?!*"

"Edmond, we didn't have time."

"You didn't have time? That's absurd. The same sequence takes place every time. *Every time!*"

"Edmond, it was your admirers," Claude followed, almost apologetically, holding himself equally culpable for this disaster.

"My admirers?"

"You were signing autographs while we were setting up and then, before we knew it, you had summoned us out with the prisoner. I told you we hadn't checked everything, but…perhaps it wasn't heard. The crowd was very loud. We couldn't even hear the priest –"

"Is that what this is about? You're going to blame my notoriety for your incompetence?!"

"Edmond, –"

"Bloody hell, the blade went halfway through the man's neck! I had to take it upon myself to put the bastard out of his misery. Do you know what that must have looked like?!!!"

"Well, yes, Edmond, we saw it," Claude replied.

"It was quite a grim spectacle," Gerard followed, redundantly.

Edmond gazed at them, his ire unrestrained. In Edmond's mind, they knew procedure. Claude had been at his side for years, after all. And Gerard, by now, was reasonably close to Leo's pace, as far as his efficiency. To Edmond, it was nothing short of a reckless oversight. They were swept up in the riotous ambience, and forgot a simple yet vital step to avert a tragedy such as this. It was stunning all the more in that, months earlier, when they had performed a test drop just prior to an execution, there had been a jam, which Edmond even noted to Ratier. Of course, it being only a test allowed them to remedy a recurrence by simply re-oiling the slats.

"Shouldn't you both be asleep?!" Edmond wailed. "You're certainly better at that than anything else. This was an embarrassment! AN EMBARRASSMENT!!! I've held this post for 15 years, and NEVER has such a catastrophe occurred under me. NEVER!" Edmond then caught sight of his shoes and, for the first time, he saw something that he had never seen on them before.

He was struck still by this, as Claude and Gerard watched him with unsettlement. "I…I have blood on my shoes. I have never, in all my years, had so much as a drop of blood on any part of my clothing, and now it looks as if I work in an abattoir!"

"Edmond, –" Claude attempted to calm him…

"And journalists were here," he whispered, as he raised his head. The blood on his shoes somehow resurrecting his newly-formed grandiloquent persona.

"What, Edmond?" Gerard asked, uncertain of what he had heard.

"They were covering this! This man killed the governor's daughter! They were all here. And look at what happened! Look at what a bloody show we put on today. Damnit, look at what…!!!"

He then caught himself. Not only were his words grotesque to him, but they were all the more so when he looked into the eyes of Gerard and Claude, who were simply unable to fathom the change in him. Edmond saw in Claude a man who said little, but knew what was asked of him. His immunity to the graphic nature of their trade made him all the more valuable to Edmond, and was something Edmond knew he could always rely upon, even as Claude appeared to be aging rapidly. In Gerard, he saw Leo, though slightly younger, and with a greater tolerance than Leo ever had towards this profession. In both, he saw their disappointment and, even more, their confusion. They only knew Edmond as a professional, with unwavering efficiency. They knew him as a man of few words, and exchanged as much with him. But what was before them, Edmond could only speculate.

Edmond looked at them, frozen by his own histrionics, before turning his focus shamefully to the ground…

"Edmond?" Claude weakly asked, having never seen an even vague display of regret or remorse from him.

Edmond remained, gazing at the soil beneath his feet,…lost.

***

15

~

In his journal, Edmond would write:

The 7ᵗʰ of September, 1913 (Paris). Admittedly, it has taken me some days before being able to document this for myself. Several days prior, just outside Le Gant Prison, I administered my 501st execution, ...with some difficulty. The catastrophe that was played out has been, unfortunately, documented in grotesque detail in the newspapers. My reputation for efficiency having now been overshadowed by something considerably less esteemed, ...though, strangely, I appear to be no less approached for my signature. What is worse is that today I was informed that Roland Marque was

Edmond stopped at this, before finally being able to admit through his pen…

innocent of the charges that were placed upon him.

Roland Marque was <u>not</u> a rapist, nor a murderer, but merely a mildly retarded indigent who was arrested due to rather haphazard policework. The female victims, most notably the youngest daughter of *the Governor, admitted to being too much in shock to make an accurate description of the assailant, and admitted so to the authorities.   However, their trepidations were ignored, in favor of an expeditious arrest and sentencing.   The result being the most brutal dismemberment of a man I have ever witnessed, all of 24 years of age. An <u>innocent</u> man.*

This fact has not been obtained by the newspapers. Nor is it to ever, according to my superiors.

I have now been privy to this information, which Minister Ratier has termed... "A life worth wasting, ...even mistakenly."

How badly I wanted to say "What is <u>your</u> life, monsieur, as you sit on your ever-widening derrière?! Why couldn't <u>your</u> face be the representative of capital punishment?!" But I could not bring myself to say a word. I left his office in a trance. Empty. Not knowing what filled me before that moment. Before that revelation. Before that execution. Before I became some sort of macabre celebrity to the morbidly curious.

Despite the public's lack of awareness regarding Marque's innocence, I feel the increasingly unsettled eyes of neighboring tenants. Better they be that than the brazen fanatics who approach me in the streets. But I can hardly consider this much consolation, for I am perhaps more unsettled with myself than anyone. Being a symbol of morbid admiration or mortal fear is to be, quite simply, inanimate.

I feel a growing insignificance in my own life. And yet, one time, not long ago, ...I felt differently.

***

He looked out the window from his seat on the Versailles-bound train, all but his eyes covered by a black face cloth. He had now resorted to wearing a veritable mask to avoid being noticed, though it had been working well enough in the recent days. Regardless, the few days in which he had been sheltered in his residence had forced him to a near madness. He could barely sleep, and the seeming few moments of deep slumber he managed would often incur visits from Father Bruneau, Roland Marque or any number of past victims. Bruneau was always the most recurring due to him being significant in the questioning of Edmond's faith. So often would his nightmares conclude with the same brooding exchange:

"As long as one's head is on his shoulders, these thoughts will remain."
"YOU ABHORRANT BASTARD! GET OUT OF MY HEAD!!!"

Edmond's wail would then sharply halt the ascending moans and the approaching shadows of the dead, as Father Bruneau stepped out from the fog in his priest's garb, with only his torso, arms and legs intact, as his hands held his head, which concluded: *"Yes, well, ...at least you still have one."*

For a man such as Bruneau, a respected man of the cloth, Edmond once had a reverence, instilled in him from his dutiful Catholic upbringing. All clergy were deemed men of God, without question. They were unscathed by the weaknesses that befell others. For Bruneau to not only kill but kill a fellow priest, especially over stolen money that he would use to finance his excursions to brothels, forced Edmond towards his atheistic leanings, which had all but engulfed what had merely been in question within him in preceding years. He knew what these criminals had done. It all the more justified his role. But as it did, it also weakened his belief in a higher power. *If we are all children of God, how do so many go astray?* was a question he often posed to himself, answered only by the next assailant. The next prisoner. The next execution. What these people had done, mostly men,…was more often unfathomable. But at a certain point, the unfathomable became the expected, and yet the clergy were to be outside of these possibilities. They would never be deemed faulted, at least to any felonious extent. But with Father Bruneau's crime came a most disturbing unveiling. No one was immune. Perhaps because, in the end, there was no God that was watching.

With the brutal death of Roland Marque, and with Edmond's subsequent awareness of his innocence, it all the more compelled him to return to Versailles to see Juliette. Through his haunting dreams and conscious depression, he ultimately saw the only thing that mattered to him. The only thing that made him feel as if his life had possibilities. He would be willing to do anything, if only he could speak with her.

He arrived at Maison's, and held his usual position at the corner of the front window, in which he would always look first to observe her beauty from afar. The store was open, but there were no patrons and no one at the counter. He knew she would eventually come out but, after a minute of waiting, Edmond decided that he could wait no more. The longer he remained crouched and covert on the sidewalk would make it all the more challenging for him to enter, as well as still risk the possibility that someone could recognize him, as had happened to tragic effect in his last visit.

He walked in, nearly shaking upon hearing the familiar bell. He stood for a moment, bathing in the still existing smells that he had not enjoyed in months, before noticing that there appeared to be less items on display than usual, especially so early in the day. He thought nothing of it, except that perhaps there was some sort of event that resulted in the purchase of much of their usually displayed inventory. But he was also struck by the pure silence. There was none of the distant ambient murmuring or metal tray clangs from the kitchen that he was used to occasionally hearing. It was as if the shop had been vacated. He looked around, praying that no patrons would enter while he was there, then gingerly stepped towards the counter, as he began to tremble, clutching his cane for stability as he awaited Juliette's entrance.

"One moment, please!" was suddenly hollered from the kitchen. It was Maison's unmistakable voice. This was even stranger to Edmond, for it was the first time he had ever not been greeted by Juliette. She was, without question, always to be the welcoming aspect of Maison's, whereas Maison himself always seemed to prefer to be hidden within the lair of his kitchen, unburdened by human interaction. It then began to cross Edmond's mind of what could possibly prompt her absence. Was she in the apartment upstairs? Was she in the park, taking a needed respite? Was she even in the company of someone else who, perhaps, rescued her from the devastation he imposed on her?

The possibilities began to rush through him, as it was becoming a bit like his dreams: overwhelming and unsettling. As he squeezed his cane, he felt an urge to leave, seeing no benefit now in exposing himself to her father. He sharply turned, and upon his first step towards the door… "Yes, sir?" Maison's voice gruffly asked, which froze Edmond in his place.

"Can I help you, sir?" Maison followed, between impatience and exhaustion.

Edmond slowly turned to see Maison, Juliette's father. He had never gotten a good look at Maison's face, but it was certainly as the voice had always indicated; aged beyond its years, but not to the point of obscuring a certain handsomeness combined with a resignation. His apron was a canvas of powdered sugar, flour and sauces old and more recent, which only emphasized his fatigue…

"Well, monsieur?" Maison followed, now appearing to take notice of Edmond's face covering.

Edmond looked at him for another moment, "I…I believe I'm still pondering, monsieur."

Maison looked at him for a moment, in turn. "Alright. Well, let me know when you're ready, then."

Then, just as Maison motioned back to the kitchen, "Is…Juliette here, by chance?"

Maison stopped, his back now to Edmond. In his pause, it seemed as though this inquiry triggered something. He turned to Edmond, his face now more a scowl. "What?"

"I'm sorry, monsieur. I was just asking if…if Juliette were here today?"

Maison then took another moment, before stepping towards the counter. He looked probingly at Edmond. "Who are you?"

"Who am…? I'm…I'm an old acquaintance,…of sorts," Edmond nervously managed.

"Not a close one, I take it."

Edmond was, of course, struck by this. He must've known something about their relationship, if not their parting, for it appeared Maison was on the verge of showing Edmond the door without further questions. "Why…why would you assume that, monsieur?"

"Who are you? Are you sick?!"

"Am I…? No, I'm…I'm afraid I don't understand – "

"Your face cloth. Are you sick? Are you contagious? You should know better than to make yourself exposed in your condition, for Godsakes. Get out of here – !"

"Monsieur, I'm…I'm not ill. I'm not sick. This is merely…"

"Merely what?"

"It's…simply intended to obscure my appearance?"

"Why?"

"I…I have a slight abnormality," Edmond awkwardly managed.

"An abnormality?" Maison asked, with skepticism.

"Yes, sir. However,…it's disrespectful for me to speak with you in this way, so I'll…remove it, if you'd let me." Maison did not give any indication either way, as Edmond waited before finally removing the face cloth.

Maison gazed at his face, analyzing exactly what Edmond could've been referring to. "Well, sir, I s'ppose the nose could be shorter, but I'm afraid I can't make out anything severe. Who are you?"

Edmond paused again, swallowed, while trying his best to loosen his discomfort as much as possible. "My name is…Edmond."

"Edmond who?"

"Edmond…de Capitoir."

Maison took a moment. "Should I know you by name?"

"Not…necessarily," he managed, with a modicum of relief.

"But you know of my daughter."

"I do, yes. Or…I did. It's been…" Before Edmond could expand, he felt obliged to at least approach Maison with an extended hand… "You must be her father. It's a pleasure – "

"Juliette is dead."

Edmond stopped, as if a wall had been thrust up to block him from moving any further. He wanted to believe he misheard. "I'm sorry, sir. She…?"

"Last month. Influenza," Maison expelled, firmly, with more resentment than sadness. The silence between them remained for a considerable moment, as Edmond could only look down at the pastries on display, still thinking any moment that she would appear. Maison was reluctant as to how much he should reveal to this stranger, but did more so seemingly out of his own need to still understand it himself. "I don't know how she attained it. Perhaps from a patron. It was rather sudden. Within days she…" His explanation faded in its significance, as he looked up at Edmond, whom he could see was unusually stricken by this.

"You had written her letters?"

This appeared to be the first words that Edmond clearly heard since Maison's revelation.

"Yes, sir, I…I did."

"I found them in her room, after she'd passed. I never read them." Maison seemed unsure what else was owed to Edmond, and normally might not have cared, but the absence of his only child seemed to compel him, after a moment: "You were in her thoughts, I believe."

"She…she had said that?"

"No. She never said much in that regard. Even less in the last several months. Perhaps it was something I just sensed. Maybe I inherited my wife's intuition or something. I don't know. I was a bit too consumed to ask at the time, since business began to slow, somehow."

Edmond could not help but feel a strong sense of guilt for this, sensing that Maison's diminishing business was likely affected by the locals knowledge of his presence, perhaps even by Juliette and he being seen together publicly. Before he could even think of words to say, Maison followed: "You hurt her, didn't you."

Suddenly, the importance of Maison's business paled significantly to this question. "Not...not intentionally. Though I...I suppose I did," Edmond answered, unable to look into Maison's eyes.

"Another lady?"

Edmond then looked directly at Maison, with an unexpected surge of emotion. "Only her, monsieur. On my life."

Maison looked at Edmond, his look of mournful judgment not wavering. "Did you love her?"

Edmond felt his reply to this question, to Juliette's father in particular, could not be rushed, or given to even the slightest misinterpretation. He needed it to be understood by him: "It is the only thing that I'm certain of," as his eyes began to moisten.

"You're rather long in the tooth for so young a woman, wouldn't you say?" Maison rhetorically inquired, very much in the manner of a woman's father who would always have a right to assess the objects of his daughter's desire. Edmond could only concur with a weakened smile. "Well, it's not considerable, I suppose. Still, I would've welcomed you. A family should only encourage growth," Maison managed without looking at Edmond. Instead, he looked about the store, as if too expecting Juliette to enter somehow...

They remained still in each other's presence; two men who were diametrically opposed physically, but who were not dissimilar in other ways. Perhaps it was their reticence with other people; a distrust, as it were. Edmond knew of this in himself, and only knew of Maison's own skepticism through Juliette and what little he observed in his visits. It was enough to make the silences between them unnecessary to fill…

"Did she tell you that she used to converse with the pies?"

"She…,yes, she did," Edmond attempted to smile at his recollection.

"She was very creative," as Maison looked at the pies on display. He then began to speak as if Edmond had left. A man with a stern façade who obviously was not willing to reveal the slightest emotional vulnerability, at least in his establishment, but the moment appeared to bring out an unusual transparency, as Edmond was still rendered immobile. "She died the same age as her mother," which prompted Edmond to look directly at Maison. "Isn't that…odd? Thirty-two years of age. So young. I've asked myself what the significance is of a mother and daughter dying at the same age, and I've come to the conclusion that there *is* none. I don't believe God, if he exists, feels he needs a reason. Perhaps He's simply…amusing himself."

They looked at each other now, kindred in their grief.

"Will there be anything else?" Maison asked, which reminded Edmond of where he was.

"No, monsieur," he barely could whisper.

But Edmond couldn't move, nor could Maison. Both were so consumed, that the likelihood of a patron walking in on them now felt all but inconsequential. The silence remained between them, before Maison gazed at a spot on the wall near the clock. It was a framed painting of Joan of Arc. He looked at it almost as if in a trance, but conscious enough to reveal what he would likely never tell anyone again: "When the English were in the midst of burning her at the stake,…it was said that an English officer claimed to have seen a white dove fly out of the flames, believing it was Joan herself, flying away, as if in a new shell. A new life," Maison tepidly smiled. "Juliette always believed that. I was raised to believe that it was not the nature of men to fathom such things, but…perhaps now, I'll consider it. What choice do I have?"

Maison, barely containing his emotions, soon faded into the kitchen without another word. Edmond watched him, still absorbing the enormity of what he had learned. He clenched his cane, alone in the middle of the shop, attempting to take in as much of the surroundings and smells as he could, for he knew he would never return.

***

16

~

On the train back from Versailles, Edmond could barely think with any lucidity. The news of Juliette's passing all but depleted him, especially combined with his lack of sleep in recent days. He gazed out the window and could see nothing but a world that held little purpose. *What has it all been for*? he wondered. Everything had been called into question now: His birth, what his trade had become, his meeting Juliette only for their love to elapse so suddenly, and now her death. Life had imposed on him a cruelty that he had never before fathomed. It was beyond a disbelief in God and the human specimens that had come before him, who committed the darkest and most reprehensible crimes.

Before long, with his fatigue and emotional containment being so great, he recalled what his brother had asked him in their last meeting before Leo and his family departed: *"Do you ever think back, Edmond?"* And with that recollection, so seemed to fade any resistance that Edmond had to return to his youth, which came to him as something between a half-conscious memory and a dream. He saw himself as a 12 year-old boy, perched atop a stool in the kitchen, as he remembered it, as his mother, Lorraine, made preparations for the evening's supper:

"Mama, can I ask you something?"

"Of course, my dear," as she carefully diced carrots.

"What does papa do?"

There was the slightest pause. "Well, Edmond, your father's told you that before, hasn't he?"

"He said that he works for the Justice department."

"Well, yes,…that's correct, Edmond."

"But…what does he do?"

"Edmond, your father works for the government."

"Yes."

"Well, there you have it."

"But what does he *do* for the government?"

"Edmond, because of the nature of your father's work, he's not able to go into much detail. You know that."

"But why?"

"Edmond, why are you asking this?"

"Does he kill people?"

With that, Edmond's mother stopped her chopping, and remained looking at the cutting board under her blade, before carefully turning to him… "Edmond, where…where are you getting this from? Where did you hear that?"

"At school."

"You should know better than to believe everything you hear from your classmates. They lie about everything."

"The teacher said it too."

"Said what?"

"That papa kills people as his job."

"Edmond, your father works for the government!" his mother abruptly demanded, which was already a rare display from her towards either of her sons.

"So he doesn't...?"

"Edmond, we're going to have our supper shortly. Now stop this! Go wash up, and I don't want to hear you speak of these things, do you understand me? All I need is Leo hearing this and, before you know it, he'll be sitting where you are, asking the same, and he's far too young to..." She looked at Edmond, as she stopped herself, knowing she had already said well beyond what she ever wanted to on this subject, at this stage in their lives. She then attempted to soften, as if to allay any of Edmond's suspicions regarding his father's trade. "Edmond, I... Your father and I had discussed that, when he felt the time was appropriate, he would sit you down and...and..."

"And what?"

Edmond was inquisitive. His mother knew this well, and was generally amenable to his curiosities. She deemed it as encouraging that a young boy ask questions as to the origin of things, the way many aspects of the world functioned. Lorraine was not uneducated herself, despite her traditional role as wife and mother. She too had curiosities, and many perhaps had subsided as she became more ensconced in family life. But the inquisitiveness of her two growing sons, she felt, was her own victory, in a way. For while their father, Albert, was always more of a staunch traditionalist, and often loath to elaborate on anything, Lorraine would encourage Edmond and

Leopold to accrue knowledge; perhaps this was ultimately out of a hope that, in so doing, they would pursue a different vocation from their father.

"Edmond,…your father is a respected official. What he does may not be considered the most glamorous profession, but it *is* a profession. And what he does is…is necessary. It helps create order and it prevents those who are criminals from…committing further deviant acts. Bad behaviors. Do you understand that?"

"Like a policeman?"

"In…in a way. But your father does something different than a policeman."

"What does he do?"

"He's responsible for making certain that the guilty are punished. It's just like in the Bible."

"How?"

"Well, you've read your bible, Edmond. In your bible, it tells you how those who commit…sinful acts must receive a sort of …discipline. Yes?"

"Yes."

"Now if the…if the offence is not so severe, in the eyes of God, then you serve a penance. Just as when you go to confession. Alright?"

"So he's like a priest?"

"Well, no," she could not help but smile at the innocence of this. "Your father's not like a priest, otherwise he couldn't be married and have children, such as you and Leo."

"Why not?"

"Well, because… Edmond, your father is not a priest, alright?"

"So what happens if someone commits a really bad crime?"

"Well,…if the offence is so egregious, so…*bad*, then…the law of God has to come into effect. Just like the law of France, which your father helps to…represent."

"Is he a lawyer?"

"No, Edmond, he's not…he's not a lawyer," as she turned back to the carrot before her…

"Then what is he?"

"Edmond, you'll find out about this soon enough,…but I don't want you to know this now."

Edmond saw a strange defeat in his mother now, as her head slouched down towards the cutting board, as if too distracted by this line of questioning to resume properly. He had thought to say nothing more, but his youthful curiosity surpassed his level of maturity. Also, he was clever enough to know that if he wanted an answer, he would be more likely to receive one directly from his mother than from his father, whom he would often find unapproachable; a characteristic which he now felt stemmed as much from the stress of his trade as from his own engrained character:

"Mama?"

"Yes, Edmond?" she carefully indulged.

Edmond swallowed, "Why does papa sometimes come home with blood on his shoes?"

"What do you mean, Edmond?"

"Sometimes…when he comes home, his shoes look as if they have drops of blood on them."

"Edmond, that isn't blood," as she suddenly began chopping a cabbage…

"But it looks like – "

She slammed the knife on the cutting board, then sharply turned to him: "Edmond, it is not blood! I've polished your father's shoes. I know what's on them. Has your father said that it's blood?!"

"He hasn't said anything, mama. I'm afraid to ask him."

"Edmond, there's nothing to be…" She stopped herself again. She wiped her hands quickly on her apron, before approaching Edmond, as if desperate for him to cease. She gently placed her hands upon his shoulders, feeling the boy who was growing too fast before her eyes. "Edmond, I've told you, your father will someday tell you everything. Alright? He'll…he'll tell you about his work and then…afterwards, you'll…you'll be rewarded with one of your favorite pastries. Perhaps a cream soufflé, with the sumptuous custard you love so much. Wouldn't that be nice, Edmond?" as she smiled widely, with a certain degree of force.

"Yes, mama. Of course," Edmond mirrored her smile, intrigued all the more as to what his father would tell him that would incur such a reward.

She brushed her hand alongside his face, embracing his silence and momentary understanding. "Alright then. For now, I just want you to enjoy being a boy. And I want you to look out for your little brother, because he's far too young to hear such things. Do you understand?"

"Yes, mama."

She looked at him for a moment; perhaps the longest unspoken moment since she had been his mother, then held his chin in her hands, which usually meant that what she was about to tell him was to be heeded without question: "My little hawk,…you have a few years left before you have to think about things that adults have to think about. And, at some point in your later life, you'll have a moment…or perhaps *many* moments…where you'll need to recall a moment from your youth. You'll need that. Those moments will give you strength and keep you warm when you feel the world is not. But in order to feel that strength and warmth from your childhood, you have to have something to look back at. I want you to have as much of that as you can,…before things change."

"How…how will they change?" he dared to ask.

And then her eyes filled, before she passed her fingers through a tuft of his brown hair… "They simply will."

"GARE DU NORD!" shouted the passing conductor, which woke Edmond, announcing his station in Paris. He took a moment to gather himself, as his car was now nearly empty. With his face covered, he managed, if somewhat shakily, to descend from the train to the platform of the station.   There he stood, rendered immobile by his mother's words from his distant past while still attempting to fathom Juliette's recent death. He looked around at the bevy of passengers, entering and exiting the next departing train, all seemingly without a care. He envied whatever they were feeling now, for it could only be an improvement on all that was within him. He was feeling an impending vertigo, of sorts. A disorientation that he had never felt before. This world that he was among was not meant for him, he knew that now. He felt his insignificance as the conductors yelled in the distance and the train whistles blew, as people raced around him, eager to embark on their quests. It all was so beyond him. He raced out of the station as quickly as his unsteadiness would permit, as he grasped his walking stick and plunged it harshly into the cobblestone with every second step that he managed…

The voices began, as his desperate pace increased:

"Do you believe in God, Edmond?" from Father Bruneau.

"No," Edmond answered, under his breath.

"Do you ever look back, Edmond?" from Leo.

"No!" Edmond replied.

"A life worth wasting, Edmond, even mistakenly," from Ratier.

"NO, DAMN IT! NO!"

"The de Capitiour blood," from Du Jonet.

"You killed the monster!" from Madame Jarnot.

"Keep your head on your shoulders – Love, Monsieur de Capitiour," from an autograph seeker.

"Juliette has passed on," from Maison.

"I want you to enjoy being a boy, Edmond," from Edmond's mother.

"To me, what you do…and what you are, is depraved,"…from Juliette.

These words would continue, as Edmond covered his ears. But nothing could block them out. They would continue, faster, and faster, and faster still…until they were atop each other, as if all the speakers were encircling him for no other purpose then to plummet him into an assured psychosis.

He eventually arrived at his destination, still tortured by the unbridled cacophony that was ascending in his head - it was the storage room of the Justice Department. He fumbled for the key, as the voices continued, before he managed to open the lock and enter the cavernous room in which his guillotine resided, already assembled,…as if expecting him.

The voices grew louder and more piercing…

"PLEASE!" Edmond begged, as he pressed his hands to his ears…

Upon Edmond's plea, the collective voices then began chanting:

"A Life Worth Wasting! A Life Worth Wasting! A Life Worth Wasting! A Life Worth Wasting! A Life Worth Wasting! A Life Worth – !

"STOOOOOOOOOOOOOOP, PLEEEEEEEEEEEEEEEEASE!!!" as Edmond fell to his knees, dropping his cane at his side. The voices, at last, ceased for the moment,…until he heard Father Bruneau's unmistakable cadence: *"As long as one's head is on their shoulders, these thoughts will remain, Edmond."*

And at last, it made sense to him. This is why he was here, after all. Why it was more important for him to come here than to his home, which now only served as a place to hide. He absorbed Bruneau's words, which he understood all too well. "Yes, I…I suppose they will," he managed to answer, under a resigned whisper.

He approached the guillotine, absorbed the entirety of its craftsmanship, rubbed his hand along the slats, where he could feel that they were well oiled. He looked at the bascule, and noted how many had lay there before their ultimate demise. It made all the sense to him that he should be the last, at least in *his* lifetime. He would slowly sit upon it, with a reluctance similar to when he would attempt to sleep. But the dreams would be gone now. The nightmarish visitations from the many who would recur in his mind would be no more. He would no longer meet Father Bruneau amidst a foggy landscape, or anyone else that would become temporarily resurrected from his journals. If it was only darkness he would see, then it would be as he had long expected. No angelic light, or St. Peter at Heaven's Gate, or any sort of postmortem paradise where souls would bathe in the joy of reunions with past loved ones. It just needed to end now.

He needed to be in a face-up position for this to work, of course, for it would be the only way that he could manage to pull the lever, which would already require considerable effort – but it could be done, he concluded. He would lay his neck within the lunette, and would then need to extend his right arm as far as he could reach, in order to give enough leverage for him to pull it down with adequate force. He was in position now, looking up at the blade, his body appropriately strewn out, as his arm extended to the lever that knew his grip all too well. He clenched it, his hand now wet with perspiration, as he braced himself for the darkness that he expected to see, and could only welcome,…before he heard it; the most unexpected sound that appeared to descend from no-where: a strangely quivering coo, along with a recurringly wafted breeze that seemed to command his attention. Since he hadn't locked the lunette around his neck, he could lift his head to see that what had landed upon his chest was…a white dove.

Edmond slowly removed his hand from the lever,…and rose ever so gradually. The dove appeared fearless and undaunted, as it moved to his lap. Edmond, now upright, continued to gaze at the bird, in disbelief of what was before him. He then held out his hands and carefully picked it up, something which he had never dared before. He looked into its black eyes, and knew that in the blackness of those eyes was not the darkness he was to soon expect. There was light in them. There was, perhaps, even love in them…

"Are you…are you…?" Edmond tried to ask without openly weeping, as tears cascaded from his eyes… "Ju…Juliette?" he asked, through a choked whisper,…before the dove would fly out of his hands and through the slight opening in the sole window. He remained sitting, looking at where the dove had just departed, certain that this was a rare pleasant dream he was experiencing. *I have to be asleep,* he wondered. It made sense to assume this, for it was beyond him to think that life was capable of such an uncanny visitation. Either that, or he was simply go-ing mad. But it would be neither. He would soon look at the palms of his hands and see the indentations from the dove's talons. It was then that he knew that this was real – and that he wasn't alone.

***

17

~

Just days later, he would write to his brother:

Dear Leo,

I hope you, Michelle and the boys are enjoying your new life far beyond your Parisian memories. I write to you with, perhaps, an unusual bit of news. I have submitted my immediate resignation to Minister Ratier earlier this week, and will soon be departing my residence of the last 12 years.

Fortunately, some savings that I had accumulated over the years has enabled me a modicum of flexibility beyond the parameters of Paris, or even of France. I will be moving to London, and taking Therese with me, of course. Yes, it's not too far. But it is a world from here, and I will embrace the distance.

There are things I would like to share with you, but I will wait until I am sufficiently relocated before expounding. I can only say that all that lies ahead for me is unknown, but I surely welcome it.

Wishing you all good health and sustenance.

Your Brother,
Edmond

***

Shortly after writing to Leo, he would vacate his apartment and board a ferry to London, where his new life would begin. His English was by no means exemplary, but it was serviceable enough. This might've appeared ample justification to retreat elsewhere, where his native tongue would at least be in proximity, but there was something about London that had intrigued him to where he felt it could be a welcoming habitat. For one, he admired its history and felt there was a certain kinship with some of the more enticing attributes of Paris. And, perhaps, it was also the unknown. And for as shy and solitary as Edmond often preferred to be, he did not want to live out his days on an island, alone. He would even later write in his journal:

While one's existence can be satiated by a blue sky and a tide's roar, perhaps there is something else.

By the time Edmond had crossed the English Channel en route to his new home, he had made the decision to change his surname to his mother's maiden name, for it now felt to be more germane to whom he was; even a rebirth, of sorts. And with such a feeling, came the uncertainty of what lay ahead.

Eventually, after having settled into a modest flat near Soho, which distantly viewed the River Thames, he would bring in his one extra pair of black shoes to a local cobbler. Edmond entered into the shop, and he would ignite the familiar bell that hung above the door. Of course, he could not help but stop at what it reminded him of, as he looked up at it, as if in wonder for a moment.

"Yeah? Whata' y'need, sir?"

Edmond was thrust out of his recollection, by way of a coarse northern cockney drawl, to see a diminutive man of not dissimilar physical characteristics to Maison; early 60s, with rough skin, slightly swelled up and weather-beaten, which only added to his sense of having lived beyond his years, donning an elaborately stained black apron.

"Yes, sir. I was wondering if you could repair these?"

"Whata' y'sayin'?" the man snipped, impatiently perplexed by the thickness of Edmond's own accent.

"Oh. My apologies, sir. My English is a bit…" Edmond then tried again, slower and with just a tad more enunciation: "I'd like these repaired, please."

"Repair, y'say?" as the man was still attempting to make out Edmond's words.

"Yes. The soles, in particular. If you could reinforce them, somehow."

The man eyed the shoes with skepticism, as he likely eyed everything. He had a considerable pile of shoes that sat behind him, of various sizes and makes, which more accurately resembled an unstable mountain of predominate leather.

"Alright, well, as you can see, I'm a bit backed up here. n'it's just m'self until I get a new assistant. So hope you're not in a rush f'these," he squawked.

"How soon?"

"Come back in two weeks n'if I haven't had a bloody heart attack by then, I'll tell ya' if they're ready."

"Alright, well,…at least I have what's on my feet," Edmond attempted a jest, but it was clearly lost on the man, who quickly scrawled a receipt and sharply pushed it across the counter: "Here."

"Thank you, s…" before Edmond could complete his sentence, the man had limped into the back, where he was no doubt attempting to forge a dent into the sizable pile. Edmond departed, still unknowing of what the coming days would bring. He would need to work soon, as his savings was not considerable enough to sustain him beyond the next few weeks. As he turned, he spotted a sign in the man's window, crudely scrawled: *"Seeking Cobbler – Inquire Within."*

Edmond re-entered the repair shop but was reluctant to approach the man again. The bell would summon him with increased hostility to the counter.

"Yes, what?!" he bit.

"I…yes, sorry, monsieur. I see you're seeking an apprentice, of sorts?"

"A what?"

"Another cobbler? Your sign – "

"Yeah, yeah. Y'know anyone, tell 'im to see me. Had a bloke quit on me last week. Yeah, y'know someone, jus' send 'im here, alright?" as the man headed to the back…

"Sir, wait. I was…I was referring to myself."

The man absorbed this, almost hoping that he was hearing incorrectly. All he could see was an immaculately dressed Frenchman of middle age who appeared to have possibly lost his mind.

"Y'self?"

"Yes."

"F'somethin' like *this*?"

"Well, yes."

"You got experience?"

"In shoe repair? No, but…I'm willing to learn."

"Willing t'learn? Ain't ya' a little long in the tooth t'want to learn a new trade? Don't y'do somethin' else?"

Edmond took a moment to absorb this, then through a weak smile, "I did, once."

"Well, what the hell happened? I mean, y'don't look like the type that needs this, sir."

"Well, sir,…looks can be deceiving."

The man gazed at Edmond in disbelief. "Y'serious?"

"Yes, sir, I certainly am."

The man continued looking at him, as if waiting for his mystification to elapse, before "What's y'name?"

"Edmond."

"Edmond. I'm Hubert, but you can call me Hubie, alright?" he abruptly held out his large and puffy hand, which Edmond gingerly shook. "Y'come in t'morra' at 6 in the A.M. and we'll start. I'll show ya' some rudiment'ry stuff, so you can at least help me cut into this bastard heap over here, got it?"

"Yes, I… That's fine."

"T'morra' at 6 A.M."

"Very well."

With that, Hubie again faded into the back, as Edmond took in his surroundings. The smell of polish was nowhere in the realm of the smells he recalled from Maison's, but there still remained something strangely kindred about this place. It felt as if he had been here before, and was somehow meant to return, at least for a time.

A few days into his tenure with Hubie, and Edmond had begun to fall into a certain pattern of lifestyle, which he was acclimating to well enough. He would work long days for much of the week, now having developed his craft slowly, but was efficient enough to enable Hubie time for short cigar breaks without fear of losing pace with his orders. Fortunately, Hubie was not one for casual conversation, unless he imbibed, which was rare. To Edmond's benefit, Hubie had little curiosity regarding Edmond's past, outside of specifically where in France Edmond came from, which would sometimes prompt a jest about the Anglo-French wars. Hubie would be more inclined to regale the air with his complaints regarding society's deficiencies: how there were few gentlemen in the world anymore, and how many of the ladies could never hold a candle to his deceased wife.

One day, he would finally ask Edmond his most probing question, as they sat across from each other, in the process of applying new soles to their respective shoes:

"Ever been married, Edmond?"

Edmond took a moment, while continuing to work. "No, sir."

"Well, I imagine y'have your reasons. T'each his own, someone once said, right?"

"Yes, I suppose."

They continued to work, as time appeared to have little resonance for either of them, and words would not uncommonly appear after hours of silence. And then, "Ever in love?" Hubie would ask, as if a hiccup more than a genuine question.

It was then that Edmond would pause, look at the shoe he had just repaired, admiring the craftmanship of his work, before taking a nearby rag to polish a scuff at the tip…

"Yes,…I most certainly was," from under his breath.

He looked at the shoe, now so immaculately polished that he could see his reflection, before the habitual silence between both men resumed.

***

Edmond would arrive at Hyde Park on the morning of his first day off in over a week. He found a bench by a pond that reminded him of the bench he once shared with Juliette back in Versailles. It had some trees that hung over it and provided a modicum of shade, though little was needed on this brisk and overcast late October morning. He set up his old painting easel, resurrected after being stored untouched in his closet for years. Painting did not come back to him as easily as cobbling was becoming relatively familiar to him now. It had been nearly 30 years since he had so much as picked up a paint brush, but it nevertheless seemed a proper time to rekindle his childhood pastime. His turtle Therese sat on the bench beside him, alongside a formidable leaf of lettuce he'd brought for her, before he raised his brush to the small naked canvas that faced him. He looked out at the pond and the browning leaves from the surrounding trees, and realized with utter certainty that it was an ill-fitting subject.

He looked at the birds that flew into the sky from the pond, and wondered if one would ever come and visit him, like the dove that visited him that day. The one who saved him.

It was then that he began painting Juliette's portrait purely from his memory of her, which would remain unwavering.

****

Daniel Damiano is an Award-winning Playwright, Actor, Screenwriter, Poet and Novelist based in Brooklyn, NY. His plays have been performed throughout many areas of the U.S., as well as London, England and Sydney & Melbourne, Austral-ia. He has been the recipient of the Christopher Brian Wolk Award for Playwriting, as well as a nominee for the Pushcart Poetry Prize and a Finalist for the Arts & Letters Prize for Drama. Among his published work is his acclaimed play, DAY OF THE DOG (Broadway Play Publishing), his debut novel, THE WOMAN IN THE SUN HAT (2021 Seattle Book Review Recommendation), his debut poetry book 104 DAYS OF THE PANDEMIC and his second novel, GRAPHIC NATURE (all published by fandango 4 Art House). In 2024, Bottlecap Press published his second book of poetry, THE CONCRETE JUN-GLE AND THE SURROUNDING AREAS, while fandango 4 Art House published his third novel, ADVICE FROM A CAT.

www.ingramcontent.com/pod-product-compliance
Lightning Source LLC
Chambersburg PA
CBHW072118300726
48975CB00003B/849